EVENTIDE

EVENTIDE

A Novel

David Osborn

Published by Dagmar Miura
Los Angeles
www.dagmarmiura.com

Eventide

This is a work of fiction. Names, characters, businesses, places, events, and incidents are either the products of the author's imagination or used in a fictitious manner. Any resemblance to actual persons, living or dead, or actual events is purely coincidental.

First published 2019

ISBN: 978-1-951130-13-8

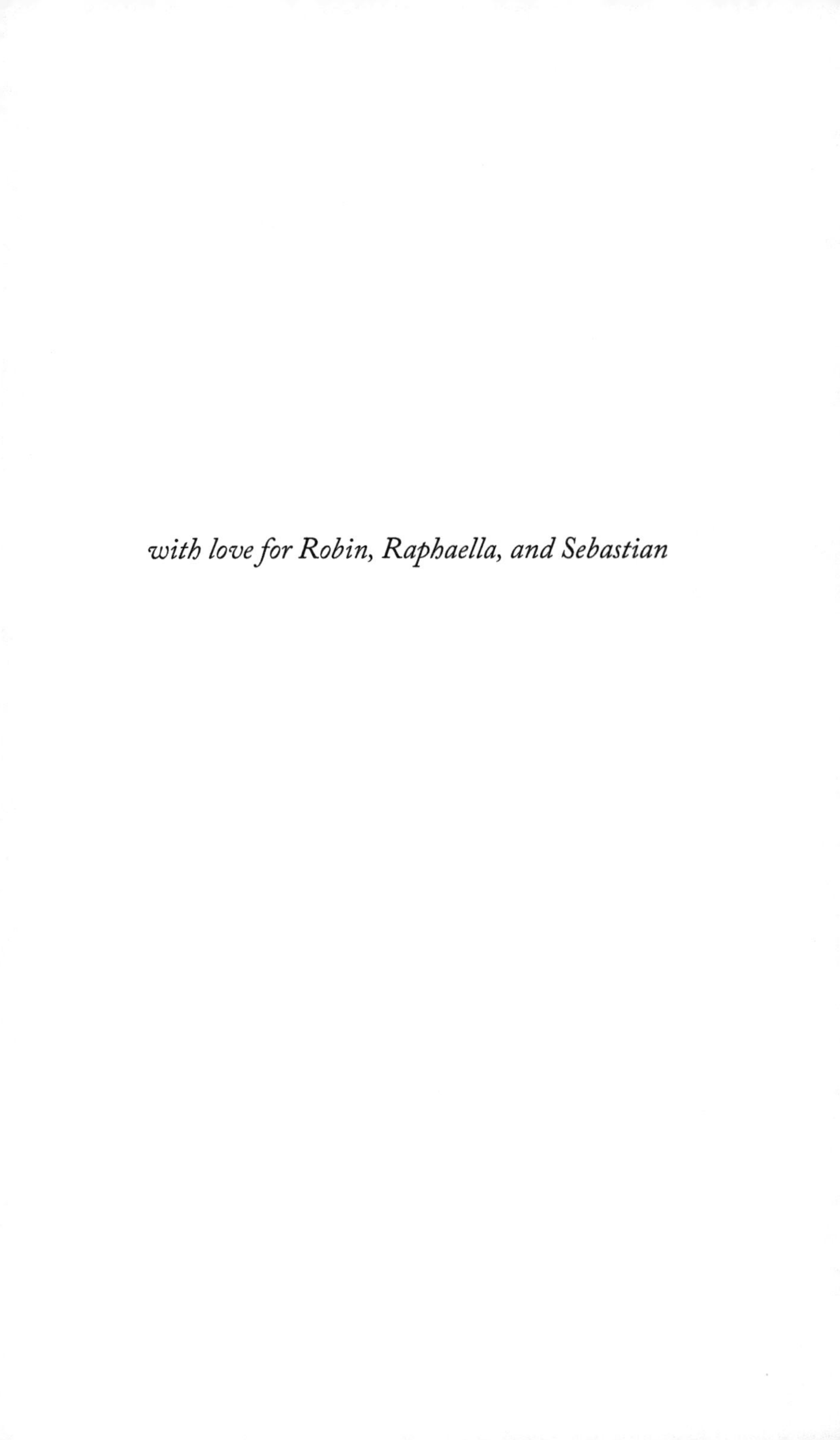

with love for Robin, Raphaella, and Sebastian

ONE

Ana Masaryk, whose once slender figure had recently, to her horror, been described as showing early signs of becoming ample, was a woman who clearly, when young, had been close to beautiful, although then, surprisingly, there'd been a rather shy look of uncertainty about her. Now, an almost severe, no-nonsense air that was quite the opposite showed in her slightly coarse graying hair, which was pulled back helter-skelter and held loosely together with several combs just above the nape of her neck. It showed, too, in the pencil jammed behind one ear, in her large horn-rimmed glasses and in her simple long-sleeved dark-blue wool dress.

At sixty, Ana was publisher and editor-in-chief of *The Chronicle,* a small weekly local newspaper in the north of New England whose logo, on the front page, displayed beneath crossed American flags, was "As local as local news can get." Besides its twelve-page front section, it also boasted an Arts section and a Business section that, combined, came to an equal length.

The Chronicle's editorial and news office, which was just off the village green of the quiet town of Union City, population seventeen thousand, shared an old two-story brick building with a dentist, an agent for an insurance company, and a podiatrist. Printing with presses long overdue for replacement was done in another building close by.

Besides the town of Union City itself, the paper served the two smaller towns of Three Rivers Junction, known locally as only Three Rivers, and Millstown, where a large brick nineteenth-century factory building, which had once turned out farm machinery, now lay idle and abandoned. The three towns, separated each from the other by several miles but linked by narrow winding black-topped roads, were surrounded, all three by a slightly rolling countryside that was part forest, part farmland; the latter distinguished for the most part not only by tall silage silos nestled against cow barns and farmyards and farmhouses but by hoary stone walls built by the early settlers to mark property lines and fence in livestock.

Here and there in the forests such walls could still be seen, amidst the trees and undergrowth, marking once prosperous farms, while occasionally visible, too, were the still standing remains of villages that had been abandoned helter-skelter when free land was opened for one and all in the West nearly two hundred years earlier, and many a farmer abandoned rocky New England for the rich fertile soil of the plains.

Serving these three small towns, *The Chronicle* left national and international news to the much larger newspaper of the state capitol and to the authoritative voices of those newspapers of the nation's major cities. It was strictly a source of local information and as such was universally seen as valuable in all three communities for its weekly news of everything from births and deaths to school sports, municipal affairs, and reports on the social activities of various clubs. Its several classified pages had long been a definite asset for all three communities with requests for, or offerings of, help with anything from home care to roofing and with "for sale" or "want to buy" notices of everything imaginable, from canoes to lawn tractors.

Editorially, it was apolitical in the sense that

it allied itself with no particular political party but liberal in that it supported human rights and invariably reserved the authority to criticize whatever abuse, whether social or economic, was perpetrated by the privileged and powerful.

In charge and responsible for all this, Ana daily began work at eight and, more often than not, much earlier. Her big oak desk, which she had inherited from her predecessor, shared last-minute articles and typescripts, a desk calendar, a long-worn leather notebook, and a roto address wheel with her laptop and an old PC.

Occupying a cramped first-floor office, a large triple-width window next to a door once commanded an immediate access and view of a much larger adjacent room and the busy activities of a near-dozen lesser souls who assembled news gathered from a wide area in and around all three towns and helped put *The Chronicle* to bed. Years before, however, Ana's predecessor, when first taking over the newspaper, had ordered the removal of the door as well as the glass window. Only the low partition below the window remained. An experienced editor, she had quickly learned, irrespective of a need for some degree of privacy, that if for no other reason than to indicate her authority, she had also to be truly in the middle of things; to be immediately available to everyone on the newspaper and in instant contact with columnists and reporters alike. That meant being within talking distance, and more often than not, her staff either legged over the partition or leaned over it—her desk was only an arm's length away—or walked unhindered through the once doorway with whatever their problem or whatever need of orders or advice.

There was no air conditioner in any part of the office. Neither Ana nor her predecessor had deemed it necessary in a place where very hot summers were virtually unknown and where, when hot days did occur, they came only a few times a year. Relief from generally stuffy air created by the paper's staff—smoking had long been forbidden—came from two casement windows that gave onto the lush grass of the village green at the far end of which could be seen the small granite obelisk which was Union City's memorial to its war dead. On a rare truly warm summer day, when even T-shirts seemed too enveloping, relief came also from a big old-fashioned overhead four-blade fan that decorated the ceiling almost directly over Ana's desk and on which, quite often, cobwebs would persistently appear during the winter months, when the fan was unnecessary.

Heat that rarely seemed sufficient was provided during the winter months by antiquated steam radiators, which Ana often delayed in turning on, preferring to bundle up against the nighttime cold that had descended on the building rather than having to listen to the annoying loud knocking the radiators made when they first began to warm up. The distraction, until the sound died to a whisper, made writing the weekly editorial, as well as one or two of the paper's lesser columns, almost impossible.

Ana's availability when she had inherited the mantle of editor-in-chief had earned her a sense of comradeship among those who helped put out the weekly newspaper. While her work requirements were often seen as tough, they were respected, and she had universally earned among her reporters, from the oldest to the youngest, the title of "boss," which was often applied with some degree of affection.

Ana hadn't always been in the business of publishing a newspaper. A once ruined life behind her and the need, as she approached forty, to securely insure with a job a whole new start on which she'd embarked, had brought her twenty-five years previously to *The Chronicle*. It was then published and edited by Ellen Brown, who had years before taken it over when an invalid spinster sister needing her care had brought her to Union City and ended her career as an investigative reporter for *The Boston Globe*.

The Chronicle at the time was nothing but

a four-page and utterly ineffective rag serving Union City only. There was neither an Art nor Business section and no classifieds. Through unrelenting hard work and newspaper know-how gleaned in her Boston days, Ellen had brought the paper close to its present state.

A portrait of her, hanging on the wall opposite Ana's desk, showed an imposing and matronly woman with a heavy jaw emphasized by a slash of bright-red lipstick that offset her pendulous jade earrings. A rather severe black dress that covered a fulsome bosom was adorned by the garnet-beaded chain securing her gold-rimmed eyeglasses. Ruling her reporting and editorial staff with an iron hand, she had, through good times and bad, steadily and faithfully supervised *The Chronicle* for nearly half a century, achieving for herself the status of something of a legend.

Another smaller frame hung on the opposite wall. It embraced a bold newspaper headline that announced in sharp letters against a blue velvet background: "Local Newspapers Are Essential to American Democracy." It shared space with a blackboard on which nearly every day Ana had the habit of chalking editorial thoughts or news that had to be amplified in that week's edition.

Avoiding the hazards of email, which included, by some, their simply ignoring it much of the time, a similar board, although cork, was in the main room occupied by the staff and had the purpose of announcing any particular orders or information that Ana wanted all member of the staff to keep in mind.

Ana's early first appearance at *The Chronicle* had been in answer to an ad the newspaper had run looking for someone to write obituaries and church news. Their previous reporter, who'd also managed the classified section, had retired, and to Ellen Brown both tasks were boring to the point of anathema. She'd drawn a line at doing them herself. Bad enough to have had to quit investigative reporting for running a small-town paper, no matter how much she had grown to love it, or how it had grown in response.

She'd at once decided she liked the look of the applicant, her slender build, her short cropped blond hair that belied her age of thirty-six. In spite of her slightly shy and somewhat restrained manner, capability was written all over her. So perhaps, Ellen thought, her twisting a handkerchief in her hands while she talked, so out of keeping with her once hazardous duty in Kuwait, then Iraq, as a U.S. Army medic, was just interview nerves.

Ellen glanced again at the application form the woman had placed on her desk when entering for the interview and at the attached honorable discharge paper from the Army along with the

Purple Heart citation. An Army combat medic? That was tough and usually frightening work. No self-effacing restraint in that, surely. So, what had happened since? Or perhaps before? More importantly and overshadowing her service, now over ten years ago, she virtually hadn't listed a single job.

"You enlisted right after college?"

"About a year after, yes."

"And the Army was for four years?"

"Yes."

Ever since entering, Ana had felt slightly uncomfortable about the way she looked. She wasn't sure how you dressed for an interview in these parts; people in Union City as well as in Three Rivers Junction were most of the time casual in their clothes. But today she had noticed on first coming in, and when she had been shown to the publisher through a weaving path among the desks and reporters hard at work, even casualness seemed to have gone overboard. Many who had just come in before her were bundled up like Artic explorers.

It had snowed heavily the day before and was bitterly cold, and she had put on heavy sweaters under her down jacket and was wearing fur boots. Noting on coming in that her interrogator had dressed in pretty much the same manner—a heavy coat hung from a clothes rack—hadn't relieved her all the way of worry about her own appearance.

Ellen studied her. Something didn't quite add up, she thought. "You haven't shown much since you were discharged in the way of employment, Miss Masaryk." Her accusatory tone also expressed surprise. "What have you been doing all these years since the Army?" She let her glasses fall from her nose to dangle against her ample bosom. "You're not twenty-one any longer."

Ana was prepared. "After the Army, I had my disability allowance due to injuries," and even as she spoke said a silent thanks to the Army for erasing from her record the ten days solitary she'd spent in the lock-up for abandoning her weapon while on a training exercise, and then, in fear of discipline for her fault, going AWOL. She'd faced a bad conduct discharge.

Now, the moment she was forgiven came back in a rush, and she saw again the stern yet smiling face of the senior officer, a full colonel she remembered, when he visited her two year later in Walter Reed Hospital. Her heavily bandaged leg was on full display as well as one arm from which surgeons had extracted a small host of shrapnel, and the nurse who had accompanied him had given him her chart to read. "Due to your war record, Sergeant Masaryk, and your Purple Heart which"—glancing at her chart—"speaks for itself, the Army has forgiven your transgression. The unfortunate incident for which you did time has been struck from the record." She had cried when he shook her hand.

Aware suddenly of her awkward silence the memory had created, and that Ellen Brown was staring hard at her, Ana rushed to stumble on, "And then I was married. My husband had inherited money and didn't really have to work, so I didn't either—well, there was a stint for a few weeks writing copy for an ad agency— and then my husband was ill for long time and needed my care."

She hadn't said that the "illness" was first the frustrating year discovering that the *inheritance* was largely imaginary and mostly money derived from gambling; then, as it ran out, her wasting fruitless and desperate years trying to stop her husband's drug habit and physical abuse while at the same time foolishly attempting to write a novel and, after giving it up, more months writing several short stories, which hadn't sold either.

"Too way-out for us," one editor had told her. And another—"It reads like you didn't really care about writing. Next one you write, try putting yourself on the line with a little defiance and taking a stand on the issues you bring up."

Mentioning any of that in the interview, Ana

had been certain, would only emphasize the failure she was.

"You're still married?"

The "no" in response was hesitant and sounded vaguely pained. Ellen decided not to press further. She suspected for some reason, she didn't rightly know why, that there had been more to the marriage than illness, but people's private lives were their own business, so long as whatever they had been, or were, didn't interfere with their work.

"You say you can write. Have you had any experience at it?"

"I edited my high-school paper," Ana lied. She had tried to sound supremely confident about the reality of such an empty working background.

Then another lie. "After the Army, I sold the occasional article for local Chicago rags here and there." And she'd added, "Admittedly that was some time ago," and had tried not to show her nervousness. In the month since, she'd realized that in the brand-new life she'd started it would be wrong of her and self-defeating not to be financially independent; she knew she would have to work. Her skimpy disability allowance through the VA wasn't enough, and she'd got nothing in the divorce except the New York apartment, which was virtually worthless because of the heavy mortgage her husband had taken on it to pay for drugs.

Getting a job, however, was something new to her. She'd been kept awake nights by not knowing exactly how to go about it. What kind of a job, and where? Working for a newspaper when she'd always been the first to criticize the media because it somehow, she thought, managed to glamorize the reality of war, was something she'd never dreamed of. Now she found even the idea of it daunting.

But here she was, just the same, and finding herself desperate not to be told, "Sorry. At the moment, you really don't quite fit, but we'll keep your application on file."

That would have left her where? Her job hunting had finally come down to either this one with *The Chronicle,* which had popped up out of the blue, or the much less preferable one taking orders behind the counter at Sally's Diner in Union City. Prior to Sally's, she'd exhausted every other possibility everywhere. She'd applied at every shop in all three towns for a position as a salesperson; she'd asked at the Three Rivers Junction hotel if they needed any additional help at their reception desk. All to no avail.

"I see," Ellen said. And to herself said, "Masaryk, Masaryk. Sounds Ukrainian. Grandparents probably, And Ana with only one *n.* Perhaps a name passed down from a grandmother. America, the immigrant melting pot …" She returned her thoughts to the interview. "You were living in New York, Miss Masaryk. Why have you come up north?"

"I wanted a fresh start in life."

"I see," Ellen said, and thought, "There must have been trouble then somewhere at some time." And aloud, asked, "How long have you been here?"

"Six months."

"References?"

"Only people at Three Rivers Junction," Ana said.

"That," Ellen thought, "meant virtually no references at all, and her past life was pretty much a blank except for her service in the Army, and you didn't hire someone just because of that, even if they had earned a Purple Heart." She owed it to herself, as well as the paper, to keep her employees up to a high standard.

"You rent or own a house there?"

"I share one."

"Oh? I know the town well. Which house? Where is it?"

"I live in the old church. Just past Sam Good's forge."

"But that's Sven Borg's place." Ellen was unable to hide genuine surprise. "The children's book illustrator."

"Yes."

"You live in the old church with Sven? Good

heavens. I've known Sven for years."

Ana had felt a slight lessening of the wire-taut tension she'd suffered since walking into Ellen Brown's office: her trying not to look so overeager as to reveal how anxious she was, nor her instant fear of the imposing and far older woman. Or was it more likely awe of the editor's fame that made her feel so painfully insignificant? Having a mutual friend was a sudden help.

"Dear Sven," Ellen said, and with a short laugh at attempted humor, added, "The town's only Swede," while wondering at the same time what an attractive youngish woman, who was desperately looking for a job, had in common with a highly successful illustrator whom everyone saw as a notorious bachelor. Masaryk! Could be a relative of some sort, but she didn't think so; surely; if she were, the woman would have told her right off.

"And such a wonderfully unique person," she added. "Last time I saw him, he was illustrating another children's book. Beautiful stuff. I remember when he bought the old church and fixed it up. People couldn't imagine that he could. But he did."

And then the lingering question she had almost hesitated to ask: "Is your sharing a permanent thing?"

The question and its implication brought a

faint half-smile to Ana's face for the first time. She thought, "Do you mean are Sven and I married, and you don't want to ask? Well, that's one I'm not going to answer. She will have to remain curious like everyone else." She said, "Permanent? Yes."

"Really!" Ellen had indeed stopped short of the marriage question. Nowadays, none of the old conventions she'd been raised with existed anymore, and it didn't seem likely; nor that a notorious bachelor had finally relented. And again, it wasn't really her business. "Whatever the relationship is there," she thought, "it was probably why the lady was applying. It was either because Sven wasn't as rich as a lot people thought, or she felt morally obliged to share expenses."

She studied Ana a last moment, feeling that there was something about her that said she wasn't really happy with herself. Or hadn't been. "I wonder why," she thought. "Perhaps she'd joined the Army to get away from something? Or somebody? Or perhaps even from herself?"

"Once more, none of your business, Ellen; not really," the redoubtable older woman thought. "You need the job filled badly. Nobody else has applied and this one looks capable."

She smiled and said, "Well, we don't need this then, do we?" She dropped the application into her wastebasket and handed the discharge and citation back to Ana. "Welcome to *The Chronicle.* If you're living with Sven, that's good enough for me. When can you start? The Union City Unitarian Church is having one of their deadly boring fund-raising suppers this Saturday. The Reverend Chorley will issue one of his long and totally predictable sermons, which have children squirming miserably until they sleep, and most adults, too. The old horror could talk a bear into hibernation. Can you cover that? Names of all the donors, the guests, what the Reverend endlessly said, and anybody else's golden words?"

A sudden and strangely dead silence.

And then: "Boss? Ana?"

TWO

The unexpected voice jarred, and with a physical start Ana realized that she had been lost in the long-ago past. She forcibly pulled herself away from being in the presence of her daunting predecessor years before and back into the present. Glancing up briefly at Ellen Brown's portrait, she pushed aside a proof of the forthcoming week's edition she had been scanning for errors and directed her eyes on a very nervous looking Clara Rosenberg. The young reporter, who covered nearly all the news at Millstown, stared back at her from directly across her desk, where she was waiting expectantly, and said, "Sorry, Boss. Didn't mean to startle you. You seemed someplace else."

Ana managed a smile. "I was," she said.

"You wanted to see me?"

"I did." Recovering, Ana was all business. "Clara, you've got Mills Garage owned by two entirely different people. Who on earth is Peter Brink?"

"My error, Boss. Sorry. Got caught behind time and was rushing it too fast. Peter's the new pharmacist who took over the Millstown Pharmacy last month when old Mr. Williams retired."

"Mr. Williams? Ah, yes," Ana said, remembering briefly the very dear white-haired old man with the rimless spectacles down at the end of his nose. He had forever smelled of some chemical or another and his hands always shook, making you wonder about your prescription, if indeed it was the one the doctor had ordered for you and made you fear, too, that he hadn't mixed the order with somebody else's.

Ana studied the young woman a moment before replying. She had dark circles under her eyes and looked thin and exhausted. It had to be the new baby. How nowadays so many of these young women managed looking after their children while working a job, too, was a mystery. But that was the time they all lived in. Fortunately for Clara, her husband was able to take breaks from running the busy Union City hardware store to mind the baby much of the time.

Clara was lucky with Craig Cotswold. Equally sharing all of Clara's household and child-care burdens, he was a first-rate young man, with a degree in architecture, who until he could establish himself was running his retired father's thriving hardware store. Other women, too many of them, had husbands still living in the dark ages and had never heard of "me too," but Ana couldn't help wondering why Clara kept her maiden name. Or was it, she wondered, what also seemed to be happening everywhere today; couples living as husband and wife, often for years and even with children, without the legal formality of marriage? It appeared that something about their independence, even themselves, would become lost by taking their husband's name; or so some said.

"All right, Clara," Ana forced the irritation she felt out of her voice. "But please be more careful, even with silly little things like this. If I hadn't caught it, we would have made fools of ourselves, or worse, made both Peter Brink and the new garage owner uncomfortable. Staff meeting tomorrow at nine sharp. Now skedaddle, okay?"

"Yes, ma'am. Thank you. It won't happen again."

When the young reporter departed and could be seen scurrying back to her desk, Ana briefly remembered interviewing her for the job nearly a year ago, and thought, "Why am I crabbing? She works hard and she needed the job when I hired her, just the way I did when Ellen hired me. Desperately, apparently. Guess that with Amazon and half the country now doing all its shopping on line, even hardware, Craig might have been struggling. And probably still is."

The name had sounded vaguely familiar to Ana when the young reporter had applied: Clara Rosenberg. Why? Odd. It had rung a bell somehow—something way back—and still did.

Ana let out what she'd been holding in: an exasperated sigh. All that aside, when would she ever have staff whose work she didn't have to endlessly review and half the time rewrite? As if both the business side of the paper and the editorial supervision weren't enough. Had she been like that when she'd started and driven Ellen Brown half crazy?

Last week young bearded Billy Hicks, known to all as "The Beard," had put two different riders on the same winning horse on the big Point to Point race out at the Sistine Farm stables. Located inconspicuously some four miles from Three Rivers Junction, the stables were owned by Archer Meyer, a billionaire horse fancier. Seeking to be free from journalists who followed him everywhere, Meyer had chosen such faraway isolation as a training ground for the U.S. Olympic team and for point-to-point open countryside steeplechase racing that annually drew thousands from all over the horsey world. Aaron Meyer, Archer's son, had phoned to bring the error, a cardinal sin in the horsey world, to Ana's attention. She had known Aaron as a little boy, when she'd first come to Three Rivers Junction, and he was affably pleasant about it, but just the same.

She spent another thirty minutes checking the week's editorial, letters to the editor, and the op-ed Martha Hunt had written about county legislation on dog restriction that would affect everyone in Union City who had lobbied for a dog park. Martha was a little more acid than she would have liked, but satisfied she could put the paper to bed while at the same time wishing *The Chronicle* had the money to go digital like so many newspapers were doing, Ana stacked it in her out-basket, ready for Johnny Wolkowski to come and get it to set type and start running the paper's old-fashioned presses in the next building.

Her desk digital clock said it was ten past five. It had been a long week and a long day, with endless last-minute changes in the paper's context and on its front page, and she was tired. Getting her key ring from her shoulder bag, slung by its leather strap over one corner of her office chair, she found a key and used it to open a drawer of the desk.

Ana was a neat person. She couldn't think in a mess. Her desk was tidier by far than the desks of most newspaper editors, and the drawer she opened was no exception. It was only occupied by two file folders, in one of which was a letter. This she extracted and then read for the tenth time. It was from Brad Jenkins of the law firm Jenkins and Barrow, and informal, as Brad was a close personal friend.

> Dear Ana: Just to more or less summarize our meeting last Friday. Reality where *The Chronicle* is concerned is that you are too close to the edge to be comfortable any longer, and through no fault of yours, are running into what small businesses everywhere are being faced with, especially local newspapers. The accountants are right, unfortunately. Revenue from subscriptions, in spite of the increase in recent years, plus revenue from advertising, which has also shown the sales effort you've put behind it, simply can't cope any longer with rising operational costs.
>
> And then there's the climbing interest rate on the paper's bank loan. I've talked to Herb Slatterly, and he says he can no longer persuade the bank's board to increase the loan even by one dollar. The Hanover Group will relieve you of the loan in its entirety, as well as underwrite all running costs, staff salaries, printing, office rental, etc. Given all that, Ana, I think you're stuck, like it or not, with accepting their bid to have you come under their umbrella.

Ana stopped reading. "Meaning," she thought, "Be no longer independent but entirely run by Hanover."

She put the letter down on her desktop and stared off at nothing. Hanover, which bit by bit had gained control over the destinies of some dozen or more other local newspapers across New England, had only recently itself come under a controlling financial umbrella: the All America First, or AAF, a giant corporation with financial interest across a wide spectrum of widely diversified endeavors that was the undisputed fiefdom of the financier Arnold Speyer, a man who was ever more and more in the headlines and on television.

Notoriously, Speyer, who operated in the law's gray area, was one who existed on the most dubious financial dealings. Pretending a certain Wall Street respectability via hedge funds and corporate ownership while forever espousing the low road of deliberately forced bankruptcies with accompanying tax relief, he had successfully enriched himself, reputedly by more than four billion.

Why, Ana wondered, had he bought into the Hanover Group? She could only think it was either for another of his bankruptcy schemes or to somehow enhance his rising political ambitions. She picked up the letter and read the answer to her question.

I know how we both feel about Speyer, and yes, he could easily run the Hanover Group bankrupt. But both the Hanover lawyers Sam Bennington and Herb

Crans, whom I've known a long time—they're first-rate guys—seriously doubt that he will do so, and they have an ear through someone on his staff—a "source" as you media people would say—to much of what he plans. He has other corporations he can ruin and dump first. So his acquisition is more likely to own yet another vehicle to spread poisonous lies and ill-conceived fabrications that would further enhance his rising political ambitions.

All told, Ana, I think you're stuck with Speyer, too, like it or not. I see no other choice, so let's try our damnedest to keep *The Chronicle* alive for as long as possible, Speyer or no Speyer. There's more at stake than jobs. I don't have to tell you, of all people, how vital small local newspapers like *The Chronicle* are to the communities they serve. Along with local government, they are what hold the whole country together, and it's tragic that they are folding everywhere.

Let me know your thoughts, Ana, as soon as you can.

Ana folded the letter and carefully put it back in its folder in the desk drawer, locked the drawer, and returned the key to her shoulder bag. If nothing else, she would insist on editorial autonomy. If it wasn't to get rich off deliberate bankruptcy, and Arnold Speyer was out, instead, to have the press enhance his political career, then let him for as long as possible spread elsewhere his sick "Take back America" ideology under the nationalistic guise of the AAF. She wasn't going to see him poison the towns of Union City, Millstown, Three Rivers Junction, and their surrounds with hideously distorted or fictitious news aided by heavily slanted photography. There were always those whores in the newspaper world, those who ran Speyer's TV and radio station, for a start, who gave lip service to honest journalism and would willingly do that for him. But she wasn't one of them.

Noise from the press room—sudden chatter, chairs pushed back, a flurry of personal activity—told her the staff were packing up and leaving for the day. It was Thursday and quitting time. The paper would be in mailboxes in the post offices of all three towns it served and on front doorsteps Saturday morning.

Someone poked their head through the wide aperture between her and everyone else who made *The Chronicle* functional and said, "Night, Boss."

And then a silence settled slowly over the newspaper's office.

Ana sat a long time, motionless and alone at her desk, again staring at nothing. Perhaps, going back before her long years of nurturing the little newspaper as Ellen Brown had done, she was remembering her first job covering the Unitarian Church function and reporting on it and on the deceased Reverend Chorley's endless and utterly dreary sermons.

The day had been a stressed-out nightmare. How awkward she had felt going up to people and asking them questions or their opinion on this or that. How embarrassed at not getting strange names straight and having to ask more than once, and sometimes so flustered that she completely forgot to write the name down. And how set back she'd been at the quite open surprise of so many at her not realizing who they were without her having to ask. Finally, above all, how frantic that she might miss something important that was routine for the job and fearful that Ellen Brown would be annoyed at her having missed so obvious a news item. She'd felt the day would never end, and interviewing the Reverend Chorley—although it was hardly an interview; he did all the endless talking while she made endless notes—had been nothing short of torture, and worse than exhausting.

Coming slowly back to the present, which for a moment the past and her disturbing first day had caused to be forgotten, she mentally reviewed the dilemma she now faced with the Hanover Group's offer. She couldn't find a ready answer.

She looked up at the portrait of her predecessor on the wall opposite. "Oh, Ellen," she whispered. "What should I do? Tell me."

The long-departed elderly woman in the portrait stared back in silence.

THREE

Some twenty-five years before that end-of-the-day moment in Ana Masaryk's life, autumn had recently begun in northern New England. Days were shortening, leaves had started to color, nights were running suddenly chill. Here and there in the early morning, a shimmer of ice could be seen on some small ponds. By day, there were the mournful cries of geese in the gray skies high overhead as they headed south, and at night, the endless monotony of cicadas.

In a long abandoned small church, known locally as the old church, which he had turned into a home on the northern fringe of the village of Three Rivers Junction, Sven Borg put the phone receiver down with a slight air of disappointment. Still in his early forties, he was a big man, raw-boned with large hands and ears, a jutting jaw like the sawed-off end of a thick log, and a prominent nose dividing bland gray eyes which perpetually protected his innermost thoughts. His Swedish extraction showed, too, in a set expression of reserve almost constantly etched on a face that seemed ever devoid of any emotional color, while all together every aspect of his makeup belied that he was an accomplished artist and a prominent illustrator.

The call he'd ended had come from a woman named Ana Masaryk to say that she had been late in getting started but that she was finally on her way, and on the parkway in Connecticut. She wasn't a fast driver, she said, but hoped just the same to be at Three Rivers Junction by nightfall.

"Where exactly are you?" Sven asked, his Swedish accent noticeable. And then, "When you get to Three Rivers, go right through town on Main Street, *ja*? And keep past the village green and the Unitarian church. I'm on the right when it thins out and just beyond a forge and a farm supply place. Can't miss me."

They had only met twice, and very briefly at that; and when she'd called the week before and reminded him who she was, it was to say that she'd had it with New York, or any big city. She wanted to tuck herself away in the country some-place, and their mutual hostess at a party months ago had said what a wonderful life he had far north in a very small town.

Sounding terribly embarrassed even to think of asking him, she had wondered if he'd mind if she drove up and had a look around and perhaps drop by and hear firsthand from him what it was like and where would be the best place for her to go.

Sven had at once offered her total hospitality. "No, no, you won't be interrupting my work at all. I'm between jobs at the moment, *ja*? So just come any time. There's a very nice little hotel in town if you want to spend several days up here." And he had politely talked down her clear discomfort at putting him out.

Now, when he left the telephone, Sven uttered a quiet, uncustomary "Damn!" He rarely used expletives, but he'd forgotten to offer his small guest room, which was partly occupied by storage, as an alternative to the hotel. People had told him the hotel was surprisingly nice, and it still had vacancies with the annual flood of tourists coming north to see the area's brilliant leaf color not yet fully underway. He wasn't sure; he hardly knew the woman, but polite hospitality, he thought, might call for offering his guest room first and the hotel second.

Hoping to make her comfortable and sure she'd be hungry after the long drive, he had bought all the ingredients for a Swedish traditional dish of meatballs with a brown cream sauce and sautéed home-grown vegetables along with a tart decorated with a pungent lingonberry jam he'd always loved in his childhood. With that in mind, he collected together his variety of food packages and, after unwrapping them, prepared to embark on a culinary effort.

Nobody knew where Sven came from, except obviously Sweden. Or why he had left Sweden, or why he had picked Three Rivers Junction to settle in. Sven was not prone to talking much, and ever taciturn, had avoided endless questions by the locals until people had tired of wondering and had simply accepted his good-natured, hard-working bachelor presence, eventually seeing him as one of themselves.

Ten years before and still in his thirties when he arrived in the town, he'd surprised people by buying the nearly derelict little three-hundred-year-old church, paying for it in cash, it was eventually learned, that he'd won in an art contest. Yielding to the village's new church, built in 1850, the little old church, as it had come to be known, had stood empty and neglected for nearly a hundred and fifty of those years. Sven, skilled with tools and solidly powerful, had methodically set to work restoring it and turning it into a simple but sturdy home with basic modern conveniences.

He had built two bedrooms, a bathroom, and a big storage closet on what had once been the altar, while the kitchen and his work room, which doubled as a living room, now occupied the large open space that had formerly seen rows of pews. His biggest job after building a fireplace and a chimney and thoroughly insulating the walls was to run a multiple-beamed ceiling across the entire interior. That shut off the peaked roofing that, unless separated, would have made heating the little building next to impossible.

Now, taking down some immaculately burnished copper pans and pots from among a dozen hanging from one of those beams, Sven immersed himself in creating his meal and thinking about his guest as he did. She'd seemed fragile, somehow, when they'd met at the dinner party, terribly unsure of herself and anxious to please and be accepted. Unusual, he thought, for such a pretty woman. His hostess had told him she'd been a medic in the Army and had done service in Kuwait and Iraq and was recently divorced. Perhaps it was just that: first shaken up a bit, and then cut adrift from someone, and feeling she no longer belonged anywhere.

When they'd met quite accidentally a second time at his publishers—she on her way out, he on the way in to discuss his illustrations for his latest successful children's book—they had chatted a moment in the lobby. When he'd asked her why she was there, she'd immediately appeared uncomfortable and had said only, "Something I wrote." She obviously hadn't wanted to talk about it or say what it was, and he'd quickly realized that whatever it was, it had been rejected. "Or perhaps she just doesn't much like me," he'd also thought, looking back at her evasiveness at their first dinner party meeting. He'd forgotten everything about her, including her name, and had been completely surprised when she had called to ask if she could drop by and see him.

The meal prepared and wanting only to be cooked, he set about putting dishes along with cutlery on the round oak kitchen table on which much of food preparation was done but that also was used for dining. This accomplished, he opened a bottle of his favorite Swedish ale he'd bought on his last trip to New York to see his publisher and sat down to await his guest, wondering as he sat in silence what it was that made her so withdrawn. It was as though she thought of herself as completely unimportant, a nobody. Sad, he thought. Everybody was somebody. He'd try to cheer her up a little. If peace and quiet and being tucked away is what she sought, she was coming to the right place. He'd have no hesitation in recommending she settle in Three Rivers Junction.

"I suspect," he'd tell her, "that this forgotten corner of the world is just the sort of town you've been thinking to bury yourself in."

✳

As small towns went, Three Rivers Junction was typical and had its own sort of charm. Why *three rivers,* nobody rightly knew, because there were only two. Indian legend had it that the Great Spirit had dried up the third in revenge for some sort of offense by the local tribe, although nobody claimed to know what that offense—bad enough to dry up a river—might have been.

Starting at the covered bridge that crossed a rushing little white-water rapid where one river was joined by another—both undeserving of being labeled such since they were nothing more than wide streams—Main Street was arrived at from a narrow, winding black-topped county road that straightened long enough to announce Simon's two-pump gas station and auto repair.

From Simon's it found a way between two lines of old buildings, some of wood construction, some of more formidable two-story brick that were typical of many a small American town a century earlier.

There was the post office, the American Union,

which was a general and dry goods store, the Same Day dry cleaners, Carol's dress shop, Ford's hardware, Pete's Lunch Box for quick meals, Dominic's grocery, and the First County Hotel, a rather grand redbrick three-story edifice with balconies and four gables that sported a Dunkin' Donuts on the ground floor next to its entrance. Several small side streets boasted a jewelry store, a shoe shop, a gift and card shop, Bill's Booze Haven for wine and spirits, and the Northern Lights, a book store, and, of course, The First Regional Bank.

All of this trailed off slowly at the end of Main Street with Dr. Carol Poster's Three Rivers Veterinarian Clinic and the law offices of Parks and Sinclair, the latter occupying a Victorian-style house complete with a rooftop widow's walk and a front porch. The town's grassy village green, still farther beyond, was graced by a granite obelisk dedicated to the dozen and a half men and women from Three Rivers Junction who over the years had lost their lives in various wars and whose names were listed on a bronze plaque sunk into its polished square base.

The street split around it, and on one side could be seen the recently built one-story glass-walled Town Hall and Library, which had won the state's architectural prize for public buildings. On the other, there were the police and fire stations. The former was the home of the town's four cops, who managed everything with only two cars, one an SUV equipped for every sort of emergency. The latter housed a brand-new fire truck that was the pride of its volunteer fire department. A rather antiquated ambulance attended by volunteer paramedics made up the town's responding unit.

As the town came to an end, one saw across some well-tended playing fields the elementary and middle schools, presided over by a venerable and bearded Mr. Perkins. High school was five miles away through rolling farmland and intervening forest in larger Union City.

And then finally, and on a rise so that it dominated the whole town, there was the classically New England church that recently had celebrated its first hundred and sixty–odd years and was the "new" church. White clapboarded and complete with cupola and spire, it was presided over by the Reverend Steven Pike, a Vietnam War veteran confined to a wheelchair, and was endlessly photographed by summer tourists. Behind it and circled with hoary stone walls was the village cemetery where some of the tombstones dated in the early seventeen hundreds.

Just beyond and when Main Street again became a weaving county road and before farmland took over once more, there was a one-story longish redbrick building of considerable age that lay parallel to the road. At one end of it, the end closest to town, the Higgins Brothers sold feed and grain along with various farm products and machinery. At the other, the building housed a forge lorded over by Sam Good, a wiry and indispensable blacksmith and master farrier of indefinite octogenarian age who was responsible for shoeing all the visiting horses as well as the twenty-five resident ones at the Sistine Farms stables.

The darkness of evening had fallen, and Sven Borg in the old church was dwelling on all of this, thinking with satisfaction that he'd found such an ideal place to work and live, when he heard the sound of a car coming off the road and pulling up before the flagstone walk that divided the grass between the road and his church home's front steps. Peering through a window by the front door, he saw, getting out of an inexpensive and ageing small vehicle, the slightly unkempt, shortish blond hair, and casual dress of the slender young woman who was at once recognizable as his guest. He rose to greet her, hoping she wouldn't find his home too humble an abode.

FOUR

A little earlier, and driving north from New York to Three Rivers Junction, Ana had left Interstate 95 at New Haven and got onto I-91. Traffic lessened after Hartford. With her entire attention no longer taken up with the heavy flow of cars around her, she was able to go over what she would say to Sven Borg when they met. As every mile went by, she felt more and more nervously uncomfortable at what she found herself doing: impulsively dropping in self-invited on the most casual acquaintance to try to get some information about the area in which he lived and about which he had painted such an inviting picture. And now, being several hours behind time and unquestionably arriving well after dark made her presumption seem ten times worse.

And then from embarrassment, her thoughts kept wandering to a nagging question as to what she was doing in the first place—driving north. Was she crazy? Was she really thinking about abandoning the apartment in New York she'd had such trouble getting in her divorce for a fantasy about a cozy secure new life in some village community someplace where she'd be able to fit in, start all over again, and not be forever haunted by ghosts of the past? Such a place, she sinkingly realized, probably was all in her mind and didn't exist. Life wasn't about places. It was about yourself. And yourself didn't change no matter where you were. Wherever and whatever that place she was headed for, it suddenly seemed in the turmoil of her imagination to be cold and heartless.

She braked so as not to be hit by a car, which in passing had cut back too sharply into her lane, even while she continued to feel the same old depressing sense of being worthless she'd always had; the obviously unwanted-one in her doctor father's household right back from when she was still a little girl and after her mother had strangely disappeared along with, she'd been told, a little brother.

She could hear her father scoffing at her when

she'd told him she planned to join the Army and was to be trained as a medic. "Had the brains," he'd said, "you were apparently never born with, you could at least have taken nurse's training first, if becoming a doctor was too much for you and if you're still foolish enough to join up."

And there'd been both their heavy silences, his and her stepmother's especially, when she'd returned from service, still on crutches from her wounded leg, the shattered thigh bone so miraculously put back together by Army doctors to be nearly as good as new, and the terrible scar made nearly to disappear entirely by a plastic surgeon.

When she came out of hospital and was still in uniform, proud of her sergeant's stripes and her row of combat ribbons along with the Purple Heart, they hadn't asked her a single question about Kuwait or Iraq, what sort of action she'd been in, what she'd seen, and only once how she'd "managed to get herself" wounded. That came from her father and with heavy sarcasm that brought from her a bitterly resentful answer. "You don't get yourself wounded, Dad. You get shot by someone, in my case a mortar round."

Nor had she been asked anything about the terror and pain of lying helpless, her leg shattered, in the midst of the fog and confusion and deafening noise of a firefight with Smiley, her medic partner blown half to bits, and the soldier she'd been tending bleeding to death beside her with her unable to help.

Coming home, it was as though she were still back in high school and later in college. The same endless put-downs, the same lack of interest in "who" she was, or "what" she was, or in any of the awards she'd won in various sports events. Nothing had changed. It was no different from what it had always been. She was the family outcast getting the same sidelining that she'd always had and which had driven her to join the Army in the first place in the hope that being in the Army would give her status. She'd finally be recognized, she'd thought, when looking at the recruitment posters. She'd be seen as somebody who counted, especially if she were to apply for medic training, which the recruiting sergeant had told her was possible. But all she'd heard, coming home, was how well her two younger stepsisters had done in college and all about her stepbrother and his new wife.

No wonder she'd gone and impulsively married Harry. It wasn't just because he was good-looking and charming and said he loved her and had asked her all about the Army; it was because he seemed to be the first person who cared, the first who had virtually recognized her very existence, and it had then taken a while to realize that he hadn't really cared at all, he'd only been talking. It had always been all about him, and it hadn't lasted long—five years only. His heavy addiction and sexual abuse had enabled the gray-haired older woman appointed by the court to be her lawyer to stand up for her and get her at least the apartment.

Her thoughts came back to the present. Was this nice man she'd met so briefly, this Sven Borg, was he only being polite when he'd told her to come on up? She tried to clearly remember how he looked. He was big and brawny and looked as solid as a tree. A tree itself, she imagined him. Or a giant woodsman who defiantly took down equally giant trees with an ax. He had a close-cropped bearded chin and a face like a block of granite. And a Swedish accent. He'd hardly had the appearance one would imagine the successful illustrator of children's books to have, or for that matter, that he could possibly be so concerned with children and could put himself into a child's imagination.

She tried to picture his home. A church? She couldn't. And the town he said was so wonderful—Three Rivers Junction. She couldn't imagine that either. She kept thinking, ridiculously, of straw-roofed shacks on stilts lining a river bank, photos she'd seen of river people in Thailand.

Sven Borg had given her the name and telephone number of the town's hotel. "Nice place," he'd said. "Comfortable, everyone says." She had called to reserve a room and hoped she wouldn't have trouble finding it. The desk clerk had said it was right on Main Street; she couldn't miss it. "Right next to the American Union, and there's a Dunkin' Donuts downstairs for breakfast." And she'd have no trouble parking. "Street pretty much clears out at night," he'd said when she'd asked if she'd have a problem with the car.

✖

She'd left I-91 and had been for some time on a state road. It was getting dark when she stopped at an intersection with a narrow blacktopped road that on her map looked very minor and had only a single, almost worn-away yellow line down the middle as a guide and which, on each curbless side, ended in woods. She saw its route sign and checked the directions he had given her. It was the road she was supposed to turn onto.

A kind of panic hit her. Again, what on earth was she doing up here? By herself on an empty road in the dark without a house or a light of any kind to be seen anywhere. And no other cars. It was scary. She should turn back, but she knew she couldn't. She couldn't come this far and then run home to New York without ever meeting the guy; she'd only make a complete fool of herself. And besides, it would be too rude for words. She had to go on. She was stuck with it, and for a moment hated herself because she was. Nobody had done it to her. She'd done it to herself; once again she'd leapt into something without clearly thinking, and because life had become too much.

But hadn't she always? It was what her family had said for as long as she could remember. She'd never amount to anything, her father said; she'd always fail, she never thought straight. It was why she'd always meant trouble to them in one way or another. And probably to everyone else her stepmother had added. "Jerk," her stepbrother had said when she'd enlisted. "You mean you actually got accepted by the Army? They'll soon find out."

Did she share some of the blame for her divorce from Harry? Everyone always said there had to be two sides to every marriage breakup. Gratefully, her older woman lawyer said that she didn't think so. Not in hers. Especially not, she'd said, given Harry's drunken rages, his flying fists, or, when sober, his sneering "You're nothing. A nonentity. Do you realize that? A zero."

Such viciousness was hardly believable, even given the smooth charming persona Harry presented to the world, her lawyer had told the judge, but it had to be believed because it was the truth. She'd clung to what else her lawyer said when it was finally all over, the warmth and kindness of her words. "Try believing in yourself, Ana. You're good and decent." Clung to it desperately.

And had clung especially to what the lawyer also said. "Ana, you need to get away. Go someplace where nobody knows you. Bury the ghosts of the past. Start all over again." She had never forgotten the support of the woman, the first person she'd ever known, other than in the Army, who had held out a helping hand. And she'd never forgotten her words.

She took a deep breath, put the car back in gear, turned the headlights on to bright, and slowly started down the empty road. She switched the car's heater on, too, because it was beginning to get cold. Winter was coming, she knew. She prayed the car wouldn't break down; it was getting so old and made so many frightening noises somewhere underneath. Like her ambulance in Kuwait when she'd driven it into Iraq.

The darkness of night pressed in against the sides of the road. There were no lights to be seen anywhere. She had never felt so uncomfortably alone. It was as though her ever-failed life had come to an inevitable end. She'd thrown it away. She kept thinking that. She'd taken her life and thrown it away, and maybe she was doing it again.

FIVE

When Sven went down the steps from his front door to the flagstone walk to the road, he found himself uncustomarily flustered and not knowing how to greet the driver as she came around the front of the car to meet him. He rarely had visitors, and at the sudden presence of the woman he'd only briefly met and who had driven up from the city, all his good-host welcoming thoughts immediately fled, and he wasn't at all sure he knew how to greet her. How should he act? What should he say? He was unable to frame thoughts.

"Welcome, welcome," was all he could think of, and then, with that out of the way and saying he hoped the drive hadn't been too wearying, he managed, "Come in, come in. It's getting very chilly, *ja?*"

She stood hesitant in the glare of headlights from the car and calling back. "Are you sure it's all right? I thought if I stopped by the hotel first it would get to be too late to see you. I mean, I know you were expecting me, but the time …"

"*Ja, ja!* Not a problem." For a moment in his confusion, Sven couldn't remember her name, but then with an inner stab of relief it appeared. It was Ana. Ana Masaryk. Her clearly once-foreign origin made him a little more comfortable.

"What about my car?"

"It's okay where it is. This isn't the city."

And Ana found herself taken firmly by the arm and led up the little flagstone walk to the front door. Enveloped by the sudden warmth of the interior the moment Sven closed the door behind them, and the night with all its anxieties and fears suddenly shut out, she felt overwhelmed. That she knew he lived in a slightly off-the-road old converted church hadn't erased a fantasy expectation of his living in the grand manner. After all, he was a famous illustrator, and wouldn't he be living very upscale amidst expensive furniture and art and modern lighting, and perhaps even with at least a housekeeper?

Instead, she found herself in the space that,

once occupied by rows of pews, now served as kitchen, living room-dining room, and Sven's workspace, as witnessed by an easel surmounted with a large half-finished illustration of two baby skunks investigating a wary turtle. A big iron pot set on an ancient coal and wood range simmered under a casserole, keeping warm a dinner, and the softly flaming maple and oak logs in a fireplace lent their burning smell to the heady lingering odor of what he had cooked.

It was as though she had somehow been transported to the safety of an almost magical world. Words seemed to come all by themselves. "Oh, Sven. How lovely."

"You like? My little Sweden in America? I have made for you a special Swedish dinner."

Ana didn't miss the pride in his voice, nor, as she looked around, the immaculate neat tidiness of the room for all of its simplicity; and afterward, the bathroom, too, where she went to freshen up from the long drive and couldn't help but notice the neatness of his shelved personal things: his comb and brush, shaving equipment, toothbrush, and the one small bottle of pills. It was so unlike the home and personal taste, or lack of it, in any man she'd ever known, beginning with her father and then certainly with Harry.

What he had cooked proved to be delicious, and while he drank his favorite Swedish ale, he had thoughtfully provided for her a wonderful vintage wine that, from her first sip, so rapidly erased some of the awkward embarrassment she'd felt on arriving that she brought herself to first compliment him on his home, asking all about it being a church and what he'd had to do to turn it into what it was now, and then daring to ask why he had come this far north; wasn't he awfully far from his publisher? And finally, becoming more daring with another glass of wine, asking about his work itself: how he had begun illustrating children's books.

The meal over, nothing would do, Sven insisted, but that they sit by the fire in two deeply comfortable chairs, enjoy each a cognac, and look at some of his recent illustrations. Completely charmed and all her anxieties and insecurities momentarily fled, Ana lost track of time, and it was with a start when an old mantelpiece clock chimed eleven that she realized she had to be at the hotel by twelve, as the desk clerk had said that they shut the doors and locked up at midnight.

That she had far overstayed her visit and perhaps overburdened his hospitality flooded Ana with instant guilt. Almost worse than barging in on his life the way she had, she had completely forgotten why she was there and had learned nothing about the region she'd come to find out about. She couldn't come back in the morning and take advantage of his kindness a second time, and she had a dismal sense of having done what she had done most of her life, and that was mess up.

"Goodness, the time!" she said in sudden panic and rose abruptly from before the fire. Her feeling of shame at having abused his hospitality so overwhelmed her that she could only barely manage to stammer her thanks and apologize for the hour. "Please forgive me," she began. "I've stayed far too long and …"

Sven cut her off quickly. "Not at all, not at all. I have much enjoyed your company, *ja?*" and raised a big hand as though to stop her from saying more. "Since we must meet tomorrow, so I can show you our town and all around, why then do you rush off to the hotel? I'm afraid you would find it quite noisy in the morning, Three Rivers gets up early."

Sven felt heat flooding his face. Was he being too forward? Perhaps she'd feel insulted. He took a breath and thought, "She can only say no and accept my apology." The words came in a flood. "And I have a very nice little guest room here. You have come such a long way, and here there is a wonderful quiet in the morning." He couldn't stop himself and rushed on. "Your suitcase is in the car, *ja?*" He raised a big hand again. "No, I won't hear 'no'. You are staying here." And before Ana could say another word, he had gone out the door to fetch it.

Completely at loss as to how to cope, Ana sank back down in her chair, her thoughts in a jumble. What on earth should she do now? And why was he being so nice? Surely, he couldn't be taking advantage and hitting on her. He didn't seem that type at all. She couldn't find any answer and, in her confusion, realized that it was too late to refuse. It would be worse than rude and awkward if she did. It might even be hurtful; he had cooked such a wonderful meal and bought a special wine for her.

When he came back she managed to stammer how kind it was of him to put her up and, unable to say more, allowed him to show her to the little guest room, with its single bed and an orange crate as a bedside table for one small lamp, and where, when setting down her overnight bag, he apologized for the boxes and things that he had temporarily stored in it, and then brought in a heavy quilt before saying good-night. "It's cold here in the north," he said, "and perhaps you are not used to it. If you want more covers, call out. I don't mind being woken, *ja?*"

The door closed firmly behind him, and she was alone. To her relief, the bathroom was directly across the hall from her. She stole to it with her toilet articles bag and found that he'd put a freshly laundered towel and face cloth on its vanity table. With it all feeling terribly strange, she brushed her teeth quickly and wiped away her eye makeup using tissue from a convenient box of them that was clearly brand-new and had just been put there.

Returning to the little guest room and sitting on the edge of the bed beneath the room's one window, where he had hung inexpensive curtains, something in her simply gave up. She was in the house of a virtually strange man just outside a totally strange town and with no connection to anything familiar. It was almost like being in the Army all over again, with no idea of what the next day would be like, just grateful to be able to fall back and get what sleep you could until whatever. The thought was oddly comforting. For all the misery and terror of war, and the humility and prior shame of being in solitary for ten days, there'd been a kind of safety in the Army she'd never found since. A silent stillness stole over her. "It has to be the wine," she thought. "I should never have had so much."

It was her last thought until with a start and opening sleep-drugged eyes, she saw that the little room she was in was flooded with daylight and that she was covered with the heavy quilt her host had provided. She glanced at the wristwatch

the Army had issued and which still kept perfect time. It was nine o'clock and she realized that
she'd fallen asleep with all her clothes on.

But the quilt? She had no memory of having
retrieved it from where he'd laid it over a chair
the night before, and she realized that he must
have come in while she slept and covered her.

SIX

Sven was cooking breakfast when, finally washed and dressed, Ana joined him. She felt all the shyness she'd always felt when confronting strangers immediately on awakening, and she couldn't find anything to say right away except "Good morning."

But any awkwardness was soon dispelled. Eggs, bacon, and toast with pancakes on the side were put down in front of her at the kitchen table, and with it a steaming mug of coffee.

And Sven, sitting across from her and beginning vigorously to put away an equal lumberjack breakfast, was saying, "After breakfast we will look first at Three Rivers Junction, *ja*? And then

Millstown and Union City. Nobody here says Junction unless talking about something official. It's just Three Rivers."

He wouldn't take no for an answer no matter her apologies, which were now less formal. She already felt as though she had known him for years and was entirely comfortable when he rather apologetically asked if it would be all right if they went in her car.

"But of course. What's happened to yours?"

"It died."

"Died?"

"*Ja.* She was very old, poor thing. And one day she just didn't want to go anymore."

"But what do you do?"

"I walk, *ja?*"

"You're not buying another car?"

A shrug. "In Sweden where I came from, we didn't need a car. Got along fine."

"But how do you get to Union City?"

"I walk."

"All the way?"

"*Ja.*" Sven laughed and Ana found herself laughing with him. It all seemed so far from New York and so utterly improbable.

With breakfast over and Sven gone to the RFD mailbox by the roadside to collect any mail, Ana went to the little guest room to get herself ready for the day. Sven had said that with autumn rushing on them, it might be chilly, so she put on a heavy sweater. Coming back, she glanced through the open door of his room. It was almost monastic in appearance, with little if any decoration, the bed perfectly made and everything else militarily tidy. About to move on, she spotted two framed pictures on his dresser, the only pictures visible, and unable to control her curiosity, stepped into the room for a quick look.

Obviously taken some years before and in Sweden, one was of a lovely young woman who in a feminine way looked remarkably like Sven. The other, taken when Sven was considerably younger, perhaps still a student, was of Sven holding hands with a handsome blond man of the same age whose head was resting affectionately against Sven's shoulder. A brother? He looked nothing like Sven.

Ana, surprised with sudden realization and immediately feeling the worst kind of privacy invader, retreated guiltily while instinctively now knowing that she would not be discomforted by any unwanted advances.

The mail collected and Ana's coat on, Sven quickly bustled them both into her car. It started with its usual reluctance, and the moment he heard its underneath rattle that had so worried her during the night when she'd driven up there, he ordered her to go at once to Simon's, giving her a store-by-store tour of Three Rivers Junction on the way as they drifted slowly down Main Street, with him especially pointing out the hotel she was supposed to have stayed at.

Ana hadn't seen much of the town in the darkness when driving through it to get to the old church. She had a sense of friendliness from the shops and was surprised and impressed by the whole area around the village green, the town hall and library, the police and fire stations, and the school with its playgrounds that was set back from everything else. The place seemed unique to her, a whole little world of its own.

When they finally got to Simon's garage and pulled up by the gas pumps, a broadly smiling Simon himself appeared from where he'd been working inside a truck when Sven shouted out for him. A dark and swarthy person, he greeted Sven like an old friend. When he heard about the noise in Ana's car, he was under it in a flash, a wrench in hand, to reappear several minutes later with the noise gone. "Loose exhaust pipe back of the catalytic converter," he said. "Not a problem."

After the stop at Simon's, they did Millstown, which Sven told her was an important agricultural center for the region. It got its name, he said, from the long abandoned mill that sat on the outskirts of town by the side of the boiling river which had provided its machinery with power. It was a big three-story brick building with rows of small windows typical of the many like it that had dotted New England throughout the entire nineteenth century and well into the twentieth.

"They couldn't keep it going against modern tools and robots and all that," Sven said. "There are plans to someday, maybe years from now, to turn it into offices and condominiums, as lots of people would like to move up here where life is not so hurry-hurry, *ja*?"

Ana could quickly see why. She easily imagined living in a condo on the top floor with a view down over the river and out over the surrounding countryside. Or shopping at a store on the ground floor, which Sven said they wanted to make into a mini mall.

The rest of the town looked thriving. It was larger than Three Rivers Junction and was spread out more, with no particular Main Street. There were more shops and stores. There were two churches near a large village green dominated by a town hall with a fieldstone exterior that was surrounded by a plentitude of shrubbery with here and there an exotic decorative tree. And although all together Millstown had its own particular charm, Ana thought that it didn't have the intimate tucked-away-from-the-world feeling that to her made Three Rivers Junction so friendly.

They saw Union City next. Some distance away, it was larger than Millstown and Three Rivers Junction put together. In spite of being close to the intersection of two important county roads and hosting a modern motel and a diner, it had a feeling of intimacy close to that of Three Rivers Junction. Its impressive village green with its war monument was almost entirely surrounded, save for a large classically New England white clapboarded church at one end and by beautiful old once-residential houses that now harbored lawyers, doctors, an antique store, and a pharmacy, as well as various other small businesses.

Sven pointed out a low redbrick building that flanked the village green. "That's the home of *The Chronicle.*"

"*The Chronicle?*"

"Our local newspaper. Comes out every week. Covers Union City, Millstown, and Three Rivers, all three: who won in high school sport, and school and community news, and fires, and police things, all that. Who is born, who has just died, *ja?* Don't know what we would do without it."

He bought a copy, and when they returned to his old church home in Three Rivers Junction, Ana looked at it while Sven made dinner again, and she was fascinated by a way of community life that she had never dreamed existed.

The governor was taken to task in the editorial for slowness in repairs on surrounding roads that were the province of the state; the girl's high school lacrosse team at Millstown had defeated Union City; a Kiwanis club meeting had raised several thousand dollars for disabled war vets; police in Union city had apprehended two men who had allegedly broken into and robbed the till of Michael's, a clothing store in Three Rivers Junction; a man with the distinguished name of Reginald Van Essex had retired from the First Regional Bank after thirty years of service. And in the art section some beautiful paintings were displayed that were the work of the mentally disturbed children at a nearby home for them. It went on forever.

The day had been tiring; they had covered so much ground, seen so much, that Ana was almost dizzy from it and didn't resist when Sven insisted she spend the night again. Sven loved horses, and while cooking another delicious dinner, he said, "There is still all the horses to see," explaining while they ate about the Olympic training stables not far away and the point-to-point races that horse lovers from everywhere came every year to watch.

Ana was too tired to resist staying longer to visit the stables. The next day came, and she met Archer Meyer, its famed multibillionaire owner, who had once come to see Sven, on learning that he was Swedish, for advice on a Swedish holiday, and gave him a warm welcome.

"If you're planning to come up here from New York," he said to Ana when he learned of why she was there, "then you've come to the right place. You can live your life in these parts without being bothered, especially with people endlessly digging into your past." The billionaire had been married three times to equally famous women, and the media were mercilessly inquisitive about anything he said or did.

. His little boy, Aaron, who took a shine to Ana, introduced her to his father's favorite horse, Copper, a beautiful giant the color of the metal that gave him his name. He then dragged her for an hour all over the lovely surrounding countryside, pointing out the difficult point-to-point jumps, stone walls and fences and streams, until she was thoroughly exhausted.

Ana had never so much as touched a horse. Horses were something she saw in movies or on TV or pulling tourist carriages around Central Park in New York. Caressing the big animal, looking into his eyes, breathing in the smell of him, and feeling the softness of his muzzle and the warmth of his breath, she felt the animal's soul somehow enter hers, and she came away with something in her changed forever. She felt in love; not with anything or anyone in particular, but with life itself, with the miracle of it existing not just in people, but everywhere and in everything.

"There's no difference between people or anything else that lives," the billionaire said. "Creatures whom we look down on and disparage as not being as good as us." And laughed and added, "And often are far better."

When yet another day passed visiting the fire and police station and meeting the Reverend Steve Pike, who although confined to his wheelchair offered to take her in hand and introduce her to any or all of the people in Three Rivers Junction; and with her helping Sven evenings with the cooking and washing up, it seemed to Ana she was experiencing something she'd never dreamed existed, even in her most longing fantasies: she was living a life she had suddenly and strangely come to feel was where she belonged. With something akin to a disturbing shock, she had begun to dread leaving it and going back to New York.

She'd come, also, to feel totally comfortable in Sven's presence. She realized she had sudden and unexpected feelings about him that she'd never had before about anyone. He was quite unlike any man she had ever known, and she found herself constantly thinking about him, wondering at how strongly masculine and competent he was. And wondering, too, why he had left Sweden to isolate himself in a small village in New England's northland, and what his life in Sweden had been like; who were his family, where had he lived and what had his boyhood been, and where had he gone to school. And finally, how he had become an illustrator.

Determined to ask him when the right moment came, she went to bed on the third night of her visit with strange long-buried feelings about really caring for someone, until she finally fell asleep, huddled warmly under the quilt he'd covered her with her first night there, while unaware that on his part Sven himself was having thoughts about her he'd rarely had about anyone before.

Living by himself in the little home he'd made of the old church, he had always been content. Or thought he was. Being alone seemed natural; it was just what life forced on you. He lived, except for the noises made by the TV, the radio, and the kitchen when preparing a meal, in a world of pleasant silence. He had a daily routine that was comforting, and his untroubled thinking was about other people, about daily chores that had to be done, and most of all about illustrations he was working on or ideas he had for new ones. There was a deep solace in work.

Now something had happened to upset all that. Quite unexpectedly, this Ana had come into his life and had aroused in him all the long-buried feelings he'd had back in Sweden for his sister, Ingebrit.

As children, he and Ingebrit had been inseparable, almost one, and later, even when she had married Olaf, they continued to fight life together, protecting one another from whatever storms came their way: Ingebrit was there for him, his only solace after Tove Larsen, whom he had had loved in secret and with whom he had planned a life, abandoned him for all that glittering world of champion cycling.

When Ingebrit became pregnant, he was as overjoyed as she and her husband. And although Olaf was a decent and good man whom she loved, she had been thrilled more for Sven than for him. "I shall be the greatest mother," she'd said, "and you, dear Sven, the greatest uncle, the guiding light in life of my little one."

Then the unimaginable happened. Ingebrit suddenly and unexpectedly died along with her child while giving birth, and something in Sven also died. Life abruptly fled him.

A great and aching loneliness, too deep to describe and which he consciously struggled to ignore, had filled his heart. Life was something forced on you that you managed the best you could. Each day was like every day, every night like every night.

Until that strange moment when Ana stepped from the car and while she stood in the glare of the car's headlights and hesitantly called back to him, something happened that took him completely by surprise. It was as though Ingebrit suddenly lived again. The life in him that was gone for so many years came back, and he'd felt a lightness that had long ago become unfamiliar. Even after their first dinner and when silently covering Ana's sleeping form with the quilt her first night there, realization that she would be leaving the next day became unimaginable, and he'd done everything he could to extend her stay and delay her absence.

Until the inevitable happened. There was a final breakfast. There were Ana's profuse thanks for his hospitality, his taking her overnight bag to her car. And finally, their standing by it and both suddenly as awkward and uncertain as to what to say as they had been on her arrival.

When it came out of Sven, it did with a sudden uncontrolled burst of painful sound in the last moment's heavy silence. "Ana, wait. Don't go."

"Sven …" Seeing his hurt, Ana fought to hold back the tears she'd felt coming herself at leaving; at leaving Sven's old church home, the safety she felt in the town of Three Rivers Junction,

66

Sven himself. The very thought since she had first awakened of abandoning what she'd always dreamed of and returning to her inconsequential lonely past had become unbearable.

"Don't go. Stay here." He waved a huge hand at the old church. "This. My home. Share it with me. You came wanting to know where there could be a refuge for you in the north, *ja?* Why not right here? Ana, don't go."

The rawness of his released emotion for a moment numbed her. She was unable to speak, even to think. She could only silently stare up at him and feel a deep aching hurt inside her.

And with that came an almost overwhelming awareness that this wasn't just the famous illustrator whom she'd met casually at a party and who, equally casual, had kindly offered to advise her about a refuge in the north. This was someone whom she had come to see differently, someone who behind the distant and formal Swedish manner and the celebrity status in publishing that had at first so awed her, was someone else entirely, someone she felt she'd always known, and was safe with, someone above all who cared and who didn't think that she always messed up, and was a failure, and had thrown her life away.

Tumbling words finally came, incoherent and unremembered but in which the meaning was clear. They said yes, she would.

SEVEN

The years rolled on with almost a blurred rapidity of endless seasonal changes— spring, summer, autumn, winter. Then spring again. In the north country, Ana was established as *The Chronicle*'s editor and publisher, and after a frigid winter and now with blossoms, which had warmed the spirits of everyone, beginning to tire and fall from shrubs and trees, the lengthening days gave a promise of summer.

At 5 a.m., Todd Bernstein, who delivered papers early Saturday mornings before high school lacrosse practice, tossed *The Chronicle* deftly onto the front porch of a Union City house from the driver's window of the beat up Chevy he'd bought at a junk yard for two hundred dollars and brought back to life himself for a hundred and fifty, scavenging for used but acceptable parts everywhere.

Driving on, he realized he was a little behind time and would have to hurry things up. He still had Three Rivers Junction to do. He shared half the town with "Acey" Don Sikeman, who was also on the lacrosse team as a defense center and had Main Street, while he had the far end of town where his last paper pitch would be at the forge of that old guy, Sam Good, who shoed horses. He often thought to skip him; it took an extra five minutes to get his paper delivered. But Good had done a few favors for his father, welding some stuff down at the fire station in Union City.

Pitching another paper at the next house along the street, he mentally went over with a silent laugh the editorial he'd read in that week's issue before starting out on his two-hour delivery round. The editor sure had a way of getting people to pull their socks up, he thought. He'd kept almost every editorial for all of that year in a scrapbook at home and planned to write his last year's final English essay about them. It might help him get into a journalism school someplace, which is what he wanted to do; he'd caught the journalism bug from reading *The Chronicle* front to back every week as well as by delivering it.

The editorial for that week read as follows:

This week we have witnessed in our own area the appalling lack of civility and respect that is sweeping our nation and which, far too often, is expressed in unnecessary loudness. Allow me to quote from the eighteenth-century English poet Oliver Goldsmith, who wrote in *The Deserted Village,* his famous lament for better times long past: "And the loud laugh that spoke the vacant mind." The phrase can be indicative, if by moving one step beyond laughter, one examines much of our intercourse today. Whether personal, economic, or political, too many seek to achieve their goal by loudness, not just in their speech but in their behavior and manners.

A case in point was last week's Town Hall meeting at Union City library when over a hundred gathered, along with several dozen or more from Three Rivers Junction and Millstown, to discuss a day's extension of the annual Shoppers Fair in which local shops publicize their wares from stalls on Main Street as part of a "Shops Make a Village" initiative, created to counter loss of business to Amazon and Walmart.

What promised to be an interesting meeting quickly degenerated into a classic example of totally uncalled-for loudness. A group of protestors objecting to any extension that would divert traffic to crowd residential areas tried to gain their point by shouting down all opposition and by adding jingoistic chants that made any reasonable public discussion impossible. Two reporters from *The Chronicle* even came close to being assaulted by several of their number.

Unwarranted loudness, whether in laughter or otherwise, and whether local or national, as unfortunately seems today's case, indeed seems to indicate a vacancy of intelligence. The protesters, in seeking to gain their point by their appallingly noisy and uncivil behavior, as bad as any schoolboy squabbling, succeeded only in bringing near unanimous disapproval against themselves and shame on the whole town.

In the perhaps vain hope that today they are embarrassed or even contrite, this newspaper avoids diminishing any such regret by not printing the names of their ringleaders.

"Schoolboy squabbling—I like that," Todd said, laughing as he tossed out another paper. "Dad will get a kick out of that one."

An hour later in the old church and with most of Three River's Junction still asleep, Ana's cell phone alarm with its soft musical rendition of "At the Beach," pulled her slowly awake and away from a meaningless jumble of dreams and vaguely disturbing memories.

Remembering what she faced that day in Boston, far to the southeast, she rose quietly and got dressed, trying not to let immediate depression at what lay ahead get the better of her while at the same time urging herself to think positively and to mentally lay out a schedule for every step of the day. She'd drop by the office first and pick up the file she'd left in her desk drawer. It contained all relevant and up-to-date financial data on *The Chronicle* along with the letter she'd received from Brad Jenkins about the proposed Hanover Group absorption of the newspaper.

Then it would be straight to the law offices of Jenkins and Barrow at Union City to pick up Brad, who said he'd be downstairs waiting at the Dunkin' Donuts on the corner. Then, after abandoning the new compact car that she and Sven had bought together when she had finally talked him out of walking just everywhere, she'd get into Brad's much larger one and she'd head with the lawyer on the long three-hour drive to Boston.

Studying her face in the mirror after showering and brushing her teeth, she silently cursed the slowly appearing crow's feet around the corners of both eyes that complimented the increasing gray in her hair. Nevertheless, she was glad she'd gone to bed early and had mostly slept well. Yesterday, with the meeting with the Hanover Group looming, she'd felt a bundle of nerves. Nothing at the paper had seemed to go right. There were always days like that, but yesterday was especially bad because Archer Meyer, still riding in spite of being in his seventies, had unpredictably died in a shattering fall at one of the point-to-point course's most dangerous jumps.

The water-hurdle at which the famed billionaire lost his life was a two-foot-wide low stone wall with a drop the far side of four to five feet into a sizeable-width brook that had to be spanned in the same jump. His horse had started to balk on the hard-frozen ground, then urged on, had jumped badly. Its front hoofs hit the wall, causing it to virtually summersault forward, and it had crashed down on Archer, who had landed half in the brook and half on the heavily tufted grass beyond.

Over the years, Ana had developed a casual relationship with the billionaire, occasionally seeing him when she visited the stables or at public functions they both attended, and she was shocked by the accident. She had wanted to write his obituary herself, to give Archer the farewell she felt he justly deserved, to mention especially how important a part of the Three Rivers Junction community he had become. She wanted it to be an obit that was far better and more appreciative of him and his life, as she and all of Three Rivers Junction had known him, than any that would appear coast to coast in the more important papers. Most of all, she wanted him to have a wonderful remembrance because he had introduced her to Copper. She had never lost the first impression she had received on first meeting the great horse, Meyer's favorite, when she had felt his very soul commune with hers; and she had every six months or so revisited him with a bunch of carrots, his favorite snack.

When in his old age and let out to pasture, he'd see her coming and with a soft knicker of pleased recognition make a slow way to her, and when he'd finished the carrots, she'd spend a half hour with him, quietly talking, her head leaning against his, her hand gently on his muzzle. If she happened to be momentarily depressed in remembering her former life, or in any way by the lack of romance in her current one, she drew from the big horse's gentle calm and love a renewed sense of security.

Completely swamped, however, by the major media calling and pouring in from everywhere in the country the moment the accident was announced, and unable to take on the obituary herself, she'd made certain it would be well written by giving it to Clara Rosenberg, who had done such a great job on Copper's when the old horse was finally gone. Of all her staff, the young reporter was the only one with the ability, good judgement, and writing talent to do justice by it. The job she'd done on the School Board Oversight Committee scandal was nothing short of outstanding and written as though she'd been in publishing a lifetime and had newspaper blood in her veins. It would help, too, that the young reporter had got along well with Archer the one time they'd met and she'd remarked about his Old World decency, his graciousness and good manners that didn't seem to exist anymore. Her relaxed manner with him had made Ana briefly feel as she had when she'd hired her, that there was something about Clara, that had a familiar ring somehow—did the young woman come from money?—but she'd dismissed the thought and hadn't wondered again.

Now Archer Meyer's son Aaron, no longer the little boy who had so attached himself to Ana years ago, would take over his father's financial empire. He was already a man with influence, power, and political clout in Washington and elsewhere, and one who would almost certainly be one of the state's next senators; Ana had developed a real respect for him. His continued presence at his father's stables outside Three Rivers Junction served to fortify that the world's seeming descent into vulgarity and hate hadn't yet, with only the occasional exception, seeped into the part of the country she had chosen to establish herself permanently in.

Other than the pressure and sadness she felt over Archer's death, she otherwise today felt surprisingly composed and determined, even fatalistic, her awakening anxiety and depression only momentary. Whatever came of the meeting in Boston, she'd fight for *The Chronicle*. It had become, along with Sven Borg, her whole life; the paper meant everything to her—what it did for all the people of Three Rivers Junction, Millstown, and Union City, how it gave them a unity, a face, and a personality. It was her responsibility to all three towns and all who lived in them who had given her a home and purpose in a new life and to long-gone Ellen Brown as well, to keep it alive at all cost.

Trying to be especially quiet so as not to wake Sven, who had stayed up late working on an illustration, she managed a coffee and a little cold cereal, hurried through both, and after writing a short note to Sven saying she was off and would be back for dinner, she tiptoed to his room and gently opened the door and peered in. He was sound asleep, his hair, now getting grayer and grayer like hers, a crown on the pillow. Her heart softened at the sight of him. It always did. Dear, kind, wonderful Sven. Like her, he was getting on in years. It seemed as though she had known him forever, that he had been an integral part of her life for as long as she could remember; a loyal and lovingly close brother she could always depend on. They occasional had their ups and downs, differences in common domestic disputes, even sometimes anger with one another; what couple didn't? But their union was as strong as ever. She could no longer imagine life without him and the world of hope he had brought her into.

It had been that way since the very first day when he had shown her all around Three Rivers Junction, Millstown, and Union City and had introduced her to everyone he thought of importance, like Simon and the wheelchair bound war-vet minister, Steve Pike, to Archer Meyer, that surprisingly friendly horse owner and his wonderful little boy, Aaron, and especially to Sam Good, the crusty old blacksmith and farrier who lived next door and was God's gift to having a neighbor, surely.

She gently closed the door on Sven and went out to the car, where she stopped a moment to take in the first rays of the now late-rising sun striking a few still drifting-about cumulus clouds left over from yesterday's rain and turning their edges a soft pink. Breathing in the cool damp early morning springtime air, she thought how lovely it was; she had never tired of living where she now lived. It was endlessly beautiful. "Almost too beautiful," she thought, "to be tainted in any way by Arnold Speyer and his kind."

She started the car, warmed it up a moment, tuned the radio onto the NPR station, and drove off.

✄

The kitchen of the small apartment above the Union City hardware store—which beside all and everything that was considered hardware, sold snow-shoes, sleds, and skis—was one of the four rooms that was home of the young architect Craig Cotswold, his wife, Clara Rosenberg, and their little baby daughter, Celine. It was a warmly pleasant place. Its walls were decorated with Spanish plates and posters of French impressionists; its one window faced east and caught the early morning sun when the light-blue drapes, drawn across it at night, were first opened.

At about the same time that Ana left to meet Brad Jenkins, the kitchen found Clara staring into a mug of coffee on the kitchen table with her elbows supporting both hands holding the sides of her head. She and Craig had killed a bottle of wine together at dinner, and too sleepy to think of clearing up and putting the kitchen to bed, they'd settled Celine, when barely able to, and had gone to bed themselves as fast as they could get undressed.

Now looking up from her coffee at the pile of unwashed pots and dishes in the sink and then at her watch, Clara guiltily thought, "Poor Craig," and hoped perhaps he'd leave the whole mess until she came home that evening; it was her turn at dishes. But at the same time, she knew he wouldn't. She'd come home and find the apartment immaculate, the kitchen sparkling, their bed made, and little Celine beautifully looked after.

When Craig stumbled in wearing his pajama bottoms and a T-shirt emblazoned with the word ARCHITECTURE beneath a picture of the Parthenon in ancient Greece, and carrying the baby, she still felt too numb to answer his "Good morning."

He got a bottle of Clara's milk she'd pumped the evening before from the fridge, put it in some hot water to warm it, and when Clara didn't look up from her coffee, sensed trouble in her, and said, "Are you still stewing about your goof?"

Waiting for the child's breakfast to hit the right temperature, he poured himself a mug of black coffee from their coffee machine and sat down across the table from Clara before she answered.

"You mean having Peter Brink run Mills Garage?" She managed a smile. "No. I was forgiven for that."

"Then what?"

Clara took a moment before answering and then said, "I didn't tell you last night, but Ana handed me the obit for Meyer."

"Really? Wow. She didn't want to do it herself? She knew the guy."

"She hasn't time for it. She's got everyone from CNN to the AP, Fox News, and Reuters down her phone line."

"So?"

"So, I'm scared stiff."

"Oh? Why?"

"Why is I'm not sure I can handle it. Meyer was a big VIP all over, not just here. It's got to be a good one, and it's bound to be *The Chronicle*'s front page and probably picked up by a lot of other papers. If I goof it, I've had it. I don't think Ana would ever forgive me."

"Oh, c'mon lover, you won't goof it. You're a damn good writer."

"Not good enough yet. But that aside, it's more than just the possible front-page pickup that scares me. What about the byline I now always get?"

"So?"

Clara's voice rose, filled with sudden tension. "So, with a whole damn world of media all over the place, and my name front and center, someone is bound to pick up on it, no?"

Craig was silent a moment. He got the baby's bottle from the hot water, tested it, began to feed her and took a sip of his coffee, and then said, "Honey, you're going paranoid again. You've been away from it for over ten years. Nobody is going to remember."

Watching him, Clara fought down irritation and said, "Craig, journalists are trained to remember."

"Yeah, yeah, sure. But *The Chronicle* and Union City are miles away from anywhere. Especially Pennsylvania. Your name now would be totally out of context from all that stuff ten years ago. You're not the 'you' that you were then. So calm down."

Clara said, "I doubt there is another Clara Rosenberg around, if that's what you're thinking, and the Clara I was ten years ago would get me fired on the spot today."

"You can't be sure of that. You said yourself that Ana Masaryk is okay. Strict but good, you said. And several times."

Neither then spoke until the baby finished her bottle, When Clara rose from the table to take her to be changed, Craig said, "Honey, why don't you stop uselessly proving your independence to yourself and drop Rosenberg for Cotswold? Are you clinging to your Daddy's famous name, or what?"

Clara instantly bristled. "Of course not. And you know better than to even think so."

Craig saw a fight brewing. Clara's wealthy background, the debutante stuff and private boarding school and all that, was a sore point even after three years of marriage and though she'd renounced it in every way many years before they'd met.

"You have the legal right to it," he said in a mollifying tone. We had a damned nice wedding, or have you forgotten?" With her family disowning her, they'd gone off with some friends to city hall, then and with only those closest to them both, had celebrated on a Long Island public beach, where they'd made one concession to wealth by drinking champagne and had roasted hot dogs and steamed clams.

Clara melted a little. "I haven't forgotten, thank you, and it's probably too late now to help anyway. I have a face, remember?"

"Yeah, I know. It was in all the scandal rags down there for weeks, and …"

"And this place is already swarming with reporters, and I'm recognizable."

"There you go again. Paranoid."

"Craig, stop. I'm not paranoid and never was, damn it."

Craig laughed. "Never was? C'mon, Clara. Your deciding that the postman was potentially an enemy because for some stupid post office reason a question came up about your former address—that's not paranoid?"

"No."

"Or when we went to that dinner the other night, that awful what's-her-name who kept dig-dig-digging to find out who and what you were before you married me and became a reporter?"

"Craig? Could we talk about something else? Celine needs changing, and I've got a big day ahead, and I'm already exhausted."

Craig knew when to shut up. He sighed and said, "Okay. Hand over Celine. I'll do her. And what shall I get ready for dinner tonight? Your choice."

EIGHT

*B*rad Jenkins was a short, square man in his late fifties with a still full crop of crew-cut blond hair that was beginning to gray at the temples. He was originally from Arkansas—"Right out of the hillbilly Ozarks," he used to laughingly say. He had done law at Columbia University in New York and had been seduced to practice in New England's far north by his partner, Bill Barrow, with whom he'd shared a tiny apartment while at school. "Sounds crazy, but I've never regretted it," he often told people who'd wondered why he'd turned down an offer to clerk for one of the U.S. Supreme Court's justices. "And anyway," with a self-deprecating laugh, "what do you expect from an Ozark boy? We're all a little *'tetched in the haid'* out there, right?"

Ana, very briefly when Sven was in New York and after too much wine, had once, a long time ago and before she'd met his wife, fallen into bed with him. Both had regretted it: Brad because he was married, herself because she had always hated one-night stands, and for a long time afterward, when seeing Brad and his wife socially—she'd found that she liked Kitty—she'd felt embarrassed and guilty and had hated herself. She'd always thought that momentary sex, even with someone you knew well, was too often giving away, gratuitously, a part of yourself. Sex had to do with really caring, or should, and one-night stands to her were nothing more than a drunken flirtation you simply were unable to resist but that often came back on you hard.

There had been other occasional incidents as well on trips to New York and with old friends she'd once dated and before she'd left her forties, although there'd been none that she regretted the way she regretted sex with Brad, not just for herself but for Brad too, because she was certain, loving Kitty as he did, that he felt even more guilty about his momentary fall from grace than she did.

On her part, her worst guilt was because of Sven. He was a brother to her, nothing more, a nonsexual man she adored and was happy to share life with. Her guilt where he was concerned was not sexual guilt but guilt in hiding from him what she was doing and where she was. Odd couple as they were, they were intimately friendly and held virtually no secrets from each other, which in some ways was the strength of their union. But still, she was a woman, and the urge for raw passion with a man occasionally surfaced and was difficult to subdue; and the upside was that she always came home feeling wonderfully a woman, one who had successful lured and controlled a man into deeply satisfying her most primitive self. Even though she knew she was probably only one of many for the men she enjoyed, her confidence would soar.

❧

She found Brad at the counter of Dunkin' Donuts and took a stool next to him, where he was already into a cup of coffee.

"Morning, Ana. All set?"

"Fully briefed and prepared to dig my nails in."

He laughed. "Especially, I take it, if Arnold Speyer shows up."

"Do you think he will?"

"Hope to God not. Seeing him once a few years back was quite enough, thank you."

"You've actually spoken to him?"

"Regrettably, and I can hardly call it speaking.

At least not by me. Speyer says what's what, and how it's going to be, and that's that. Any dissension or protest, no matter how right or how reasonable, is greeted by stony silence."

"Which means it's Speyer's way or nothing at all, right?"

"Right. And whatever his high-handed pronouncements, ninety percent is guaranteed to be what he's famous for: either pure fabrication, outright lies to cover up illegalities, or concocted accusations against people who are on to him."

Ana laughed. "Don't tell me. I caught him on the TV last week in a town hall meeting where he was pushing his political agenda. Dodging the interviewer's every question with an aggressive attack on either the interviewer or whomever had aroused his displeasure, which meant everyone except possibly the pope, and promising a chicken in every pot, so to speak, to all the poor loyal suckers at the meeting who were screaming support when they can't see that what they will actually get, if anything at all, will be stale cold cuts."

Coffee finished, they were soon on the road south, and as they began to travel on major highways with all the incumbent heavy traffic and with far more evidence of business and population buildup on each side of the road, Ana was glad that she wasn't driving and even more so that she now lived where she did, away from any heavily settled areas. Although she'd started the day energetic and determined, what she saw out the window was a reminder that they were on their way to a big city, and total reality set in that sooner than she would have liked—she'd shortly be at the rather dreaded meeting with Hanover.

Neither she nor Brad Jenkins spoke further for a while until Ana finally broke the silence. She said, "You intimated that unless it's another bankruptcy scheme, Speyer's only real interest in gaining control over Hanover with his AAF All America First bunch, might be to amplify his so called political 'America For Americans' nonsense."

"Correct. Not simply one of his contorted get-Speyer-rich financial deals. He could use the relatively wide demographic spread of the Hanover Group enhanced by *The Chronicle* to spiel out the one hundred percent propaganda he does with the AAF."

Ana tried not to visualize Speyer, his shiny total baldness that gave him an almost unpleasant phallic look at odds with his sparse, always beautifully tailoring, his air of austere authority compromised by narrow merciless eyes, which along with an ever-unsmiling expression seemed always to project a fixed unwillingness toward any compromise. She said, "Brad, it isn't his autocratic attitude before any TV camera or microphone; I could stomach that where we are concerned. It's his appalling record of saying one thing and doing precisely the opposite, of ignoring the views and advice of his own lawyers, that to me is his real danger."

"Well," Brad replied, "if there's a deal actually to be confirmed, we'll try our best to get a contractual guarantee that where any area news covered by *The Chronicle* is concerned that he doesn't do that."

"Cross fingers." And then, "Brad, how much does he actually know about my *Chronicle*'s finances? Are we not stuck with a weak hand?"

"Depends on how much he's been able to pump out of your accountants and Herb Slatterly. Accountants, probably nothing. Slatterly? It's anybody's guess. Like too many bankers these days, Herb would sell his soul to the devil if there was a buck to be made and unctuously justify his doing so. As though the million he's already got through so-called 'wealth management' wasn't enough. Worshiping the folding green all through one's life as an almighty god-the-father, god-the-son, and god-the-holy-ghost has the odd effect of seriously warping one's moral core, if one ever had one to begin with."

Ana laughed, reflected, and said, "Herb sometimes reminds me of an officer back in my Army days. He'd funnel money for medical supplies into his own pocket for whatever, like ingratiating himself with everyone at the officers' club by seeing that all their drinks were on the house."

"I'd forgot you once did a stretch in the Army."

'I haven't," Ana said.

Mention of the Army triggered another wave of memories in her, and she found herself laughing inwardly at how totally different her running *The Chronicle* and a possibly confrontation with Speyer was to her service in Kuwait and Iraq as a medic, when faced by last-ditch Iraqis and all those awful following days, first in a field hospital in Baghdad's walled green zone, then in the hospital in Germany, and then at Walter Reed in Washington: all the pain and confusion. She could hardly remember it now.

And finally, all the depressing homecoming business with her family. Where were they all now? She'd cut loose from the past when she'd driven up to Three Rivers Junction all those years back. When someone had somehow found her with news of her father's death, she hadn't gone to his funeral. At the thought of driving down to New York from her refuge in the home Sven Borg had created in the abandoned old church, something in her had rebelled, and rebelled so violently as to stop thinking for a long time of any part of her once-ruined life and of any person connected with it.

More of the past, however, suddenly came back. Only vaguely could she remember her real mother. A face she couldn't define, time-blurred. And warm hands, a soft voice—had there been a slight accent of some kind?—dark hair. She'd never known what had happened to her. She had been, and then simply wasn't any more.

Had there really been a brother too? That also was a blank. But then, Ana reflected, at the time she'd only been three or four years old. Her father, when she was older, saying her mother had run off with another man had always seemed a lie, and probably was, but it had shut the door forever on her finding the truth or where her mother had gone, even though she had secretly tried. There had been no living close relatives to her mother, and distant ones could barely remember her and were of no use.

Like losing her mother, so much of her early life had also always remained a half-repressed blur: school and friends, slowly and painfully growing into a woman on her own. Had she purposefully buried it the way Sven had tried to bury his? Or had she actually been innocent most of the time of what was going on around her? She would probably never know, she thought, with a wry inward laugh. And anyway, did she want to? No. Not really. Her life was now. Not the past. Her life was Sven and Three Rivers Junction and *The Chronicle,* and more immediately today with Brad and their meeting with the Hanover Group and possibly Arnold Speyer if, for some sick reason, he decided to show up—gloating in advance, perhaps?

The thought brought her out of the mist of the past and into thinking of work, and she began mulling one particular news item over in her mind, trying to put together all the facts as they had been given to her yesterday about the law suit in Millstown between a Mr. Herman Fox and a Mr. Mark Target. It had begun with an aggrieved Mr. Target claiming a constant incursion onto his property of unwanted trash caused by Mr. Fox's annual leaf blowing in the fall and then his spring cleanup months later. Apparently, this issue couldn't be peacefully resolved with Mr. Fox finding a way to keep his debris on his own property, but it got worse when Mr. Target wouldn't agree to Fox's offer to cross over the line between them and blow it back, and then went one regrettable step farther and sued.

Clara was covering the story, and next, according to her write-up, an eight-foot-high fence Mr. Target had last week gone and erected between himself and Fox was causing such an outcry with neighbors saying it was a blight on the whole neighborhood that the Town of Millstown had entered the fray with an injunction on Mr. Target to take the fence down. Mr. Target had chosen to ignore it, so that the town was now suing him.

Two lawsuits over nothing but getting rid of unwanted leaves in the fall and winter debris on a lawn in the spring. Ana found herself laughing out loud, it was all so utterly ridiculous. Wasn't there a cool head anywhere to resolve it all through peaceful arbitration? She'd write an editorial about it tomorrow suggesting such and warning that all the divisive uproar being caused in Millstown threatened to spill over into Three Rivers Junction and Union City.

She heard Brad say, "You were laughing. What's funny?"

"Work," she said. "Stupid things going on at Millstown. One thing leading to another until things get out of control. Like a snowball rolled around in wet snow getting bigger and bigger."

She focused on where they were and saw they had virtually arrived at their destination. They were coming off one of the main roads leading into Boston through the suburbs, and there it was, dominating a small business and commercial park, the imposing big glass building that housed the Hanover Group.

She pulled down the windshield visor and, using its mirror, began checking her appearance. "Human nature awry," she thought. "With newspapers, there's always something crazy happening."

NINE

While Ana was arriving in Boston, two unexpected things occurred, one in Three Rivers Junction, the other mostly in Millstown. Both were to seriously affect her.

The first concerned Sven. When she left that morning, he was woken by the front door closing and the car starting up, and it took a moment to realize that it was okay, nobody was stealing the car; it was just Ana leaving for Boston. He rolled himself out of bed, bones aching. "Not getting any younger," he thought. He got himself dressed slowly and remembering what he had to do that day.

There were two small illustrations to finish, but more importantly, he had to repair the clapboarding under the gutter that a woodpecker had been consistently drawn to and drilled. Woodpecker drilling on a house usually meant one thing: carpenter ants that came boisterously alive with winter's end. The joisting of the old church behind the clapboarding was old enough without being eaten.

Dressed and shaved, Sven whipped up some pancake batter, cooked a dozen pancakes on a large flat iron griddle pan, and after pouring himself a mug of black coffee, sat down to eat breakfast while briefly glancing over the two illustrations sketched the night before on an art pad that he'd left on the table. One was of a little girl speaking to a small assembly of woodland animals, the other of her holding the paw of a little skunk while both she and the skunk looked up at an owl, which was reading something to them from outside his home in a tree.

They were to illustrate Ana's latest story in their mutual very successful Ophelia series: short fairyland adventures for younger children. Sven smiled, remembering back to the first one, which now with others stood framed and on prime display in the bookcase to one side of the fireplace across the room.

He and Ana were having breakfast, just like

he was now, when quite suddenly and out of the blue she'd said, "Ophelia."

"Who?" He'd been quite startled.

She'd laughed. "Ophelia. A lovely dog I knew once when I was a child. I think it belonged to an aunt. I was very small. I thought that if it was okay by you that I could try to make up a little story using the name, not for a dog but for a little girl who lives in the forest with her widowed woodcutter father. She's been granted by fairies, when born, the magic of being able to understand and talk to all the woodland animals ..."

She had broken off, blushing, Sven remembered, as though thinking, "Did she dare?" And then had said, "Sven, if you thought it was any good, would you consider illustrating it?"

He could not have been more delighted. "Illustrate one by Ana? How wonderful." And he hadn't hesitated. "You and me together, we create something? Writer and illustrator like one, *ja*? Hurrah!"

It never once occurred to him that her story and how she wrote it might not be any good and that he might have to face the awkward pain of telling her honestly that he couldn't find a way to illustrate it. He took it as a matter of course that it would be wonderful. Miraculously, it was.

She had dashed the first one off the next day, wondering, she told him when he had shouted his approval, why it was suddenly so easy for her to write when it had always been so terribly hard.

The story was simply titled *Ophelia.* He had rushed to illustrate it and then to send it off to his publisher, Kinderbooks, who found it as charming as he had. That was the beginning of a successful series, with Ana coming up with another story, then another, when she wasn't overloaded with work at *The Chronicle;* and then only when she felt like it and when he, on his part, wasn't under obligation to illustrate the work of another author.

Breakfast over, Sven put any further thoughts of Ophelia aside. He washed up the dishes and the griddle pan and his coffee mug and went outside. "In ten minutes, it's done," he thought, first eying the offending woodpecker-pierced clapboarding high up on the steeple wall of the old church, then getting a tall ladder from his tool shed along with a wrecking bar, a hammer and saw, and a length of clapboard with which to replace the injured clapboarding he'd rip off.

With spring virtually over and summer promising, it was a lovely day to be outside and not chained to his drawing board. The skies were clear, the forest that Sven could see from high on the ladder rapidly greening. And like many artists, Sven took delight in practical work on home or property. It gave him a chance not to think but to give his mind a rest from intense concentration that was often exhausting. After he'd made the necessary repair, Sven thought he might take a walk, pass by Sam Good in his forge and chat a while before taking a turn around town to pick up the groceries he needed for dinner that night. He'd then get back to work on his art pad and finish up both the illustrations, which were for the fourth Ophelia book.

But high on the ladder and when he had pried loose the offending clapboard with the array of woodpecker drilled holes in it, he found to his dismay that fate had laid other plans for his morning. Not just one but several clapboards had been badly damaged by ants. Four sections, at least, had to be replaced, along with some joisting that needed to be reinforced where the ants had also feasted.

With a sigh, Sven set to work. First: Turner's lumber yard to buy half a dozen six-foot lengths of clapboarding, some two-by-fours for the joist repair, a bundle of insulation to jam between the joists, and a short roll of tar paper to tack over them before he replaced the clapboarding.

Next: the hardware store to pick up a bottle of Glop. This was a jellylike substance that ants loved and that would kill a whole colony of them in minutes, many even before they could carry drops of it back to their queen.

Doing the rounds and carrying the heavy burden of all his purchases back to the old church, he found himself laughing inwardly—carpentry, it had once been his life. Back in Sweden his father was a carpenter, his uncle a carpenter, his grandfather too. And before he had fled Sweden, he had been one also for a spell.

That had come to an end that day, which now seemed so very long ago. He'd been on the bus that took him from near his home on the outskirts of Gothenburg to one of the docks of the great seaport where he'd been sent to buy a fish at the fish market for a special meal for his grandfather's birthday. Lost in drawing a cartoon of some fish in aprons and chef's hats clustered around a large pot on a stove from which a lobster was trying to escape, he'd been accosted by the passenger sitting next to him, an elderly bearded man who peered at the little illustration over spectacles that slid down to the very end of his nose. "You are an artist, boy?"

"No, sir. I am a carpenter."

"I am sorry, boy. You are an artist. Not a carpenter. You should be illustrating books, not sawing wood. Books for children is what you should be doing."

Sven had simply smiled and remained silent. He hadn't told the man that he was forbidden by his father to draw or sketch. "All that fancy drawing, boy, is for the godless, not for the likes of us. We are tradesmen," was his father's edict in dismissing art.

But the seed had been sown, and later—how many years? Three, five?—art had won. Defying his angry father, he had run a plane down a last piece of wood, brushed the shavings onto the floor of their work room, neatly put away the plane he'd used, along with some other tools, and ignoring his father's shouted threats and anger, had walked out defiantly.

With little if any knowledge of publishing, of where to go, whom to see, he had visited a bookstore, bought a children's book, and with the blood of Vikings in his veins had boldly and fearlessly gone to the address of its publisher, printed on one of the first pages. His rough woodsman-like appearance, his blunt and badly educated self-introduction, and ignorance of anything to do with publishing brought smiles, even ill-concealed laughs, to the editors he was reluctantly shown to by a startled receptionist.

But the laughs stopped when they saw the sample illustrations he had prepared the day before for the text of the same little book. His drawings vastly excelled what was already in the book's pages.

Almost at once, he was taken on by the prestigious publisher to illustrate another children's book, and within a year after its publication in Sweden he received a substantial offer for a book from an American publisher, and with its publication, an award from an art group. He'd happily left Sweden and had never looked back. Liking the forests and farms of northern New England, so different from the crowded streets of Gothenburg, and welcoming the relative isolation, he had wandered about to finally settle in Three Rivers Junction when he saw the possibilities of a home in the old church.

Now, with all he had to do, it was well into the morning, then, before Sven was back up the ladder, and nearly lunchtime before he'd come close to nailing into place the last clapboard, sealing the offending colony of ants within the old church along with the Glop, the entire bottle of which he had emptied between the joists.

Down the road a short way, Sam Good felt ready for lunch. He had shoed three horses that morning, one skittery and dangerous, and he felt it in every bone of his body. Then there was the old iron door for a brick incinerator the town used to burn records that were no longer of use. Over the years it had rusted away. Besides doing the horses, he had forged hinges to weld onto the new door he'd fashioned from a sheet of heavy iron that, using a welding torch, he'd carefully cut to fit. Lastly, there'd been the set of door bolts he'd fashioned for Chief Bernstein at the fire department in Union City, and whose kid, Todd, delivered his newspaper.

Enough was enough. He turned down the blower into his open charcoal brazier that kept the coals white-hot and which he used to heat and bend shoes to the right size, and remembered the pie Ana had baked and given him before taking off, she said, for Boston. It was her way of thanks for his lending Sven a heavy-duty bolt cutter.

God bless her, was his thought. She was such a welcome neighbor. He liked big Sven, a good man; everyone in town liked him. But Ana was something different and even better. From the day she first appeared—how many years ago now? He couldn't remember—she'd been like a breath of fresh air, always ready to help, always neighborly and smiling. He'd never learned where she came from, nobody did, and she'd never said. She was just like Sven. Nobody knew what his past was either. But she had to be well-educated. She wrote children's books with Sven and she was the editor and publisher of *The Chronicle*.

He went into his kitchen that backed onto the forge and fished the pie from the refrigerator along with the ham and cheese sandwich he'd put together last night, and took both out front with a can of soda along with a copy of *The Chronicle.* Its news was mostly about the Memorial Day parade in Union City last week, and the editorial featured an old friend, Joshua Abraham, whom he'd known and admired since he was a kid and Joshua had gone off to fight the Germans, one of a dozen or so from the high school that year; when was it? 1941? 1942? He'd been only ten and too young to go, although he wanted to and had felt guilty because he couldn't.

He opened the newspaper and read for the fourth time what Ana had written, saluting Joshua and others, some of whom had never come back.

This year's Memorial Day parade, participated in by all three towns, Three Rivers Junction, Millstown, and Union City, was held in Union City and led by the venerable Sgt. Joshua Abraham, United States Army, whose name as well as his faith echoes that of the biblical giant. Mr. Abraham, who participated nobly in a wheelchair pushed by Rachel, a granddaughter, is a veteran of World War II. A tank commander in General Patton's Third Army, he battled the enemy from the beaches of Normandy all the way across France and into Germany, where he was the first American into one of the infamous death camps and whose ready facility with Hebrew was a blessing to those few inmates he found alive. Besides a Purple Heart and numerous other decorations, his uniform jacket, which he can still slip into, in spite of his advanced age of ninety-seven, is honored, with a Silver Star, the Army's highest award for bravery after the Medal of Honor.

Mr. Abraham bears scars for his sacrifice for all Americans. He lost both a leg and one hand from wounds received in a final assault against last German resistance. But this was not all. Like so many of our veterans of combat, he lives his every hour with painful memories of the death and destruction that he witnessed and participated in. What he keeps to himself and quietly suffers daily is beyond the imagination of most of us whose freedom and liberties he fought to protect and which we far too often take for granted.

We owe an immeasurable debt not just to Joshua Abraham, but to all veterans of our many wars and of many faiths who, regardless of whatever mindless prejudice they face at home, proudly wore their county's military uniform with all the perils and danger to their persons which that uniform all too often subjected them to. We of Union City, of Millstown, and of Three Rivers Junction must never forget that we are a nation of immigrants, one devotedly built over the past four centuries by people of all color, all faiths, and of all personal orientation. We must face, as Joshua faced the Germans, any attempt by any misguided minority to tear down the rights and constitutionally established privileges of all and everyone, regardless. Memorial Day and veterans should remind us, as we thank them for their service, of who we are and who, whatever the odds, we should continue to be.

Sam put away the paper. The good lady really felt deep for vets and what they carried, he thought, and he remembered vaguely Sven telling him Ana had done a stretch herself in the Army, so perhaps that was it; she knew from experience, maybe.

It had grown pleasantly warm, and Sam,

sitting with his lunch on the wooden bench that had once graced the lawn of the old library before they'd built the new one, shielded his eyes a moment or two. The bright outdoor light was sharp after the shadowed interior of the forge, where in spite of modern electrically operated saws, drills, and a big turning lathe, nothing much had changed since his father had worked it forty years ago. He glanced up the road toward the old church and saw Sven high on the ladder working. "Good day for it," he thought.

He was thinking about Archer Meyer dying and wondering what kind of an obit Ana would write because she would surely want to write it herself. He wondered too if it would affect his shoeing business—he thought perhaps not. Archer's son, Aaron, had taken over several years ago—and he had bitten into his sandwich, the pie awaiting its turn on the bench beside him, when he thought he heard a loud crash someplace.

He ignored it; he was always hearing noises, most of which were meaningless. Almost through his late eighties, his half-gone hearing belied his still muscular and wiry body that in spite of mornings like today could still withstand a hard day's labor with both shoeing horses and whatever was needed about town in the way of ironwork.

He'd gone on eating when he happened to glance back at the old church again, and it took a moment for it to register that he didn't see Sven or the ladder leaning against the high steeple clapboarding, and then that the two-story ladder was on the ground with Sven lying next to it.

"What the hell," Sam thought. "Sven?" There was no answer. "Holy mother …"

Sam dumped his sandwich and ran as fast as his old legs would carry him up to where Sven lay and bent over Sven's twisted body. "Sven?" And then, "Jesus …"

He bolted back to the forge, where he'd left his cell phone on a work bench, and called 911. "Sam Good," he said to the woman who answered. "Three Rivers Junction. Main Street, just beyond the library. Guy's fallen off a ladder. Yeah, lying on the ground unconscious and one arm broke to hell."

Alerted, Sally O' Donnell, the young volunteer paramedic who was stationed that day at the office of the volunteer fire department across from the town hall, ignored the ambulance as not worth the wait starting it. She shouted at Charley Gibson, the duty driver that day, to start it up, grabbed her kit and sprinted the distance to Sven. She was a second year medical student who had taken an EMT course in first response procedures the year before. While she quickly registered Sven's heartbeat and noted his pulse and got him covered with a blanket, she put in an urgent call to Charley

Gibson, the duty driver that day for the Three Rivers Junction ambulance, garaged at the fire station.

It took what seemed forever, although less than three minutes, for Charley to start up the ambulance and get it moving to the old church. Together, he and Sally stretchered Sven—not easy; Sven was a big man—got him inside the ambulance, and were off to the small thirty-bed hospital in Union City.

As they started, Sally, seated by a deathly pale and silent Sven, ran an IV saline into his unbroken left arm and keyed the emergency room.

"Looks like a fracture of the right scapula, a compound of the humerus also, and most likely a concussion. He fell from a high ladder. That's bad enough, but I'm seeing worse. I'm seeing a possible more than 5.5 plus abdominal aortic aneurysm—my guess—that might have given him a dizzy spell and caused the fall."

When the one resident doctor in Union City's hospital got the report, he ordered the ambulance to head instead directly to the helicopter landing pad on Union City's village green and called at once for the helicopter on duty at the big regional hospital that by car was over an hour away.

Making the call, he said, "And tell your pilot to break records."

✶

Long before Sven fell and at about the time Ana left to meet Brad Jenkins, Clara Rosenberg diapered her little daughter and turned her over to her husband, who would bring her down to a playpen filled with her toys and to a cot he kept in the back of the hardware store, where she would spend the day. In a small refrigerator there were several bottles of her own milk, pumped the night before and all ready for her, along with some beginning soft foods with a little silver spoon Craig's mother had given them when Celine was born. There was also a hot plate on which to heat water to warm everything. Craig had become adept at running the store and being a father, and fortunately for both him and Clara, Celine was an easy baby.

When Craig had gone with Celine, Clara pulled herself together and cleaned up the kitchen mess before quickly showering and brushing her teeth, and, after a dash of eye makeup and combing out her short tousled crop of dark hair, she hurriedly dressed in her normal workday clothes—jeans, moccasins, a T-shirt, and since it wasn't all that warm yet, a light denim jacket. She then went directly down to their old Toyota parked out front on Main Street.

Buckling herself in and starting up the motor, she thought about Craig carrying on the night before about what he called her "paranoia," and she thought, well, maybe she was, and if so, it wasn't because she didn't have every right to be. As far as she was concerned, ten years erased nothing in the way of danger.

But glancing at the front of the hardware store, and seeing Craig already putting out garbage cans, mailboxes, and a lawnmower—outdoor items that could sell that day—her heart softened. Maybe Craig was right too. It was at her insistence that he and she and the baby lived in the cramped four rooms above the store. "It's far safer," she'd said. "No prying neighbors like if we lived in a small house with only a fence between us and Miss Nosey-Parker or whomever it might be."

"You're being paranoid," she remembered Craig saying. And then the same old saw he'd dragged out ever since. "You keep forgetting that you're miles from anywhere here."

That had been the beginning of all his paranoia accusations. "Just realistic," she'd replied. "Where I'm concerned, distance means nothing, and you know it. Not in this day of Facebook and Instagram and all the twittering that goes on."

He'd reluctantly agreed on the little apartment. Craig was a practical and steady person and embraced the plus side of their living, which was his being only a short flight of rent-free stairs above his hardware store where he shared work with his employee, Tony Pinetto, a once railroad engineer who'd lost an arm in an accident. Besides that, it made it far easier with her being away all day working and his having to look after the baby while he too worked.

With the sun finally up, it was getting rapidly lighter, and a few people were seen here and there. A new day had begun. While the car warmed away the night's light chill with its inadequate heater, Clara got her heavily used reporter's notebook out of her shoulder bag and briefly ran over the short list of what she had before her that day. There was an interview first off with David Polaski, the Millstown fire chief, about a fire in which one of the volunteer firemen had been injured. Next, she had a meeting with the lady who represented the branch of the League of Women Voters and hoped she could remember her name in time; she was a notorious busybody married to a selectman. And after, her interview with the contractor who was involved in plans for the many-years-awaited restoration of the big abandoned mill building.

She also had to see the school superintendent about the middle-school graduation ceremony in two weeks and get the names of those graduating; and there was the need to throw some embarrassing budget questions at the head librarian over the proposed addition to the town library. Finally, she needed to get a copy of the town budget from the town clerk, who was the key to everything and everybody in Millstown; and then with all that seen to, she'd need to just scout around to nail anything that had come up overnight or that she hadn't picked up on the day before.

Above all, there was the damned Archer Meyer obituary to write. She'd have to fit it in somehow here and there during the day when she had a few minutes to spare, like at lunch, or in brief stops after finishing notes on an interview and preparing for the next one, then polish it up that night at home.

She was going to be on the run all day, but not the way she'd been when she'd first been hired for the job. Back then—how long ago now? A year at least—every hour had been sheer panic, and writing up news had kept her up half the night nearly every night. Two months in, she'd been a physical and emotional wreck, and it had been only Craig's tolerance and help that kept her going.

And Ana's. Looking back, she wondered why the "boss" had ever hired her. She hadn't had any recommendation from anyone except from the kind-hearted social worker who had disguised his real role with a false title of assistant manager someplace, and she'd lied and said she held a brief job as a teacher without ever saying exactly where. She'd only been able to present a truly bona fide and excellent college record.

Now, however, things were finally different. She rarely screwed up any more, like getting the names of people mixed; she was turning in good work, most of it with hardly a word or punctuation mark edited that she could see when she read her bylined article in print. Save for the occasional justified reprimand, there was Ana's often pleased smile when she turned in a story along with her "Well done, Clara. We'll make a reporter out of you yet." *Out of you yet*, meaning, she knew, that Ana thought she already was.

Ana had been especially pleased when she had turned in as a front-page story an obituary on Copper. It was far more than just an obit about a horse. It was an intimate and warmly loving memorialization of an extraordinary being that happened to be a horse, and about whom Ana often spoke of and clearly adored, and whom she often drove out to visit with a bunch of carrots when the horse, his jumping days over, had been put out to pasture.

When Ana had read the obit, it was clear how much she had loved the horse, how in some mysterious way her feeling for it transcended Copper being an animal or Archer Meyer's favorite ride. There had been tears in her eyes and her gentle "Thank you, Clara," erased any reprimand she'd ever handed out.

More important than any of that, Clara realized, she'd begun really to love the job. She'd found her niche in life. As a reporter, she was discovering all sorts of interesting people, men and women who were far more down-to-earth than those in her family background or subsequent life before Craig. She was constantly uncovering, through meeting ordinary everyday people, the most extraordinary personal stories—some tragic, some sad, many inspiring, almost all dramatic in one way or another. People you'd never suspect, she'd discovered, were a bottomless pit of unfolding drama, and there were often some with true-life stories that were or had been incredibly exciting.

Most importantly, she was discovering, with a kind of surprised awe, that heart was more important to a happy life than fame or position, and certainly far more important than money. As long as one had a comfortable roof over one's head, a bed to sleep in and three meals a day, and, most importantly, someone to love and be loved by, nothing else really mattered. Why hadn't she always thought that way? She didn't know, except that time forever seemed to erase so much, except what you didn't want to remember.

Satisfied that she was well organized and feeling good about it, she put away her notebook and, catching his eye, waved at Craig, who was putting more things outside the store for display. Pretty soon, she thought, with an uplifting surge of hope and happiness for him, the words written across the shop's front window behind him wouldn't any longer be Union City Hardware. They would be Cotswold Architecture. Only last weekend Craig had told her he was finally getting close to quitting hardware. He'd had talks with the bank and his father, and the plan was to sell out all the store's merchandise but keep his father's property as his first place of architectural business.

Pulling away from the curb for the five-mile drive to Millstown, she had to swerve into the middle of Main Street to avoid a big black sedan car parked too far from the curb as she went, wondering as she did whose car it was. She didn't recognize it as belonging to anyone in Union City, and quickly chalked it up to some guest at the motel just down the way. "Motel ought to request patrons to park in their lot in back," was her thought. Passing *The Chronicle*, she waved at bearded Billy Hicks and Helen Hunt, who was heavily pregnant, as they headed for the office to clear up whatever before setting out on their daily rounds, and a moment or two later she was out of town and on the county road to Millstown.

Arriving, she collared her first subject, Fire Chief David Polaski. She found him in the Three

Star Diner having a start-up coffee and pumped him about the fire the past week and the injured fireman. "Just a minor arm burn," Polaski said. "Over the fence gossips made it much worse. But we couldn't save the house. There was a strong wind and the damned thing burned to the ground. An electrical fire started it. We think mice in the kitchen wall chewing up wires. You might want to talk to the owners. Retired couple. They're pretty busted up. Staying with the Belchers, last house down on Firth Street."

Clara filled a page in her notebook with specifics, noted the distraught couple for a visit late that afternoon or first thing tomorrow, and then, thankful that she'd remembered her name at the last moment, she talked to Margaret Witherspoon, the woman who headed the League of Women Voters. She quickly found herself confronted by a dry acerbic woman in her fifties who knew better than anyone about almost everything and who had never adapted to the relatively easy dress habits, nor the relatively easy lifestyle, of those who lived in any of the three northern towns. A rabid and frustrated activist for the rights of "the common woman," as she put it, she clung at the same time to a fashion that was more uncommon and Fifth Avenue, New York, than L. L. Bean, northern New England. Her regular dress—she almost never wore pants or a pantsuit—was usually the latest in vogue and scaled to make women of her age appear more youthful. She clung to immaculate make up, boasting that no one had ever seen her without it, not even her husband, and, more often than not, she wore stiletto heels, of all things, when they were clearly inappropriate.

It was one interview, Clara thought gratefully when finally clear of her voluble subject, during which she hadn't had to work to get answers. In fact, she'd hardly got a word in edgewise with Mrs. Witherspoon, who saw herself as an authority on every subject imaginable, speaking volumes that had to do with the League of Women Voters as well as increasing women's rights in Millstown and elsewhere.

She was coming out of the library where they had met when, with something akin to slight shock, Clara saw the same black sedan she'd had to avoid when pulling away up Main Street in Union City. Warning bells instantly told her it could be trouble. She tried to laugh off her fear. "Come on, girl, cool it. Just because you saw the same car twice. Has to be just some tourist taking it all in."

She went on to her next interview with the contractor. It took longer than she thought, and it was close to lunchtime when she finally shook hands with the man and headed back to the diner for a sandwich and coffee, taking a rolled-up blueprint he'd given her that showed quite accurately the precise conversion into offices, shops, and residential condos of the long-idle big nineteenth-century building that, along with a twin building destroyed years before in a fire, had given Millstown its name.

She had started across a rubble-strewn lot from the old mill's once active loading bay when she saw the car again, parked now on the road by the lot, and another stab of deep-seated fear turned instantly into a different emotion. Anger. Years before she had met Craig and had settled into quiet married life and a good job, Clara had been known for her temper. About certain things she still had the shortest of short fuses, and being harassed was one of them. Harassment, she was dead certain, was what that car meant. A kind of white-hot fire filled her whole being.

Rolled-up blueprint in hand, notebook secure in her shoulder bag and the bag hugged tight against her ribs, she stormed straight for the sedan. It had shaded windows that hid the interior, and she furiously pounded on the one on the driver's side, and screamed, "You in there. Open up. And right now." She pounded again. "Are you deaf? Open up."

She had bent to pick up a stone to slam against the glass when the window slowly rolled down and she found herself looking at a middle-aged man she could only describe to herself as a shoe-salesman type, indistinguishable both in clothes and face.

"You're following me," she shouted. "Why?"

There was no answer. The driver stared straight ahead in silence and that told her everything. She was right. He'd picked her up in Three Rivers Junction and followed her here.

"You sick son of a bitch," she said. "How would you like to show up in court on a harassment charge? I have friends in the town hall here. Follow me again, you rotten horror, and your next stop will be the police station."

With a faint humming sound, the window rolled back up.

"Bastard!" Clara screamed, and struck the closed window again. The sedan abruptly pulled away, forcing her to jump back to avoid having it roll over her foot. Rummaging frantically about in her shoulder bag, she got out her cell phone to take a picture of the car and its license plate, but she was too late, and after watching helplessly as the car disappeared, beyond the mill's gates, she went to her own car.

For a moment, sitting behind its steering wheel and fastening the seat belt, she couldn't think logically, but then she started to, and when she did, something akin to a deep-seated long-held fear replaced her rage, and stopped her from putting the car in gear and driving off.

Someone harassing wouldn't follow her from town to town. A harasser wouldn't be waiting for her virtually outside her home. How would he know that was where she lived? Or Millstown a place where she worked?

This man wasn't a harasser. He was following her. Yes, but why? Her fear grew deeper. And for what reason? Who would want to know way up here who she was and what she did now for a living? Her past began to roll over her like a black cloud, and she suddenly went cold all over. She had never felt so vulnerable.

A little more than ten years before this, the late-afternoon rally in a suburban outskirt of Harrisburg, Pennsylvania, had started innocently enough. Held outdoors late on a Sunday afternoon in front of a neighborhood high school, it had been billed well in advance. Nothing about it seemed threatening to law and order, and there was scant police presence. "Bunch of stupid lefties letting off a lot of hot air," one senior cop had grumbled. "Who cares?"

A cloudy sky that promised eventual rain didn't deter the several hundred supporters of the progressive FAIR (Future Alliance of

International Forums) gathered to hear speakers and to rousingly encourage the global principles and ideology they believed in. Some of those were local, some from northeastern states other than Pennsylvania. All wanted to hear important statements affirming their own beliefs from members of the out-of-power party. One speaker was an important congresswoman, another an outspoken official of the former administration. The rally was being covered by regional TV with a nationwide hookup standby, as it was one of many that day, some far larger in numbers, that were being held all over the country in protest at new White House executive orders that would further limit the right to apply for citizenship of the many millions of illegal immigrants in the country. In its very nature, the rally was steeped in anti-racism, and its supporters were a rainbow of races and LGBT supporters, along with a scattered representation of several labor unions.

Among those assembled and carrying a tightly furled umbrella as defense against the promised rain was Clara Rosenberg, the twenty-year-old daughter of a former well-known socialite senator who was now a highly paid and outspoken lobbyist for coal and oil companies and one whose politics, catching national attention and reeking of "class" and once elitist dominance, were virulently anti–alternative energy.

Clara, early on in life and an only child, had balked at being relegated to being a passive daughter not allowed first to ever have her own way, then, later, to think for herself. Increasingly, as she grew older and more politically aware from listening to and absorbing the bare facts about coal and oil's contribution to the destruction of the atmosphere, she rebelled against her father's lobbying. Occasional disagreements turned into often angry and fiery arguments, with Clara more and more alienated from her father, who in turn saw her as a disappointing betrayal and an embarrassment.

She got little help from her mother. During the twenty years that had passed since Clara's birth, Donna Rosenberg had bit by bit surrendered herself totally to the will of her dominating husband, all her thinking and ideas becoming a virtual carbon copy of his.

By the time Clara had completed an exclusive girls prep school, during which she was endlessly reprimanded for her outspokenness on nearly every subject on which she had differences with the teachers, she developed into an ever-strident, somewhat noisy, and thoroughgoing activist. At college, she joined any and every group whose purpose was protest and, college behind her, was dismissed without reference from several jobs for railing against bosses with whom she disagreed.

Both parents, shocked by what she had turned out to be, virtually closed their door to her, and this rejection seemed only to increase her activism. She became quite well known for her energy and spirit by a number of important progressive organizations, where she endlessly volunteered, and on the day of the rally at Harrisburg, she was perhaps more fired up than ever.

The rally progressed according to plan. Signs and placards were evident by the score, and the two speakers had aroused the feverish passions of the crowd when Clara, uninvited and carried away by the moment, leapt onto the podium and grabbed the mike from a startled master of ceremonies, who had little chance to object as a number of people in the crowd, who knew Clara's activism well, cheered her on with shouts—"Let her speak!" "You tell 'em, Clara!" And "Go for it, Clara!"

Clara didn't disappoint them. This was her moment; it was as though all the thoughts and differences of past years, at home as a child, in prep school and in college, welled up in one explosive moment. Her passion caught fire as, mike in hand and striding back and forth on the podium, she underscored the rally's objectives.

In moments, the crowd responded more excitedly than it had to the two scheduled speakers. Angry agreeing voices rose everywhere, and it was the roar of sound that the crowd made that was perhaps the reason that nobody noticed the arrival of a large group of neo-Nazis and white nationalists until it was too late.

It was not until the first rock thrown, the first bucket of filth dumped over an unsuspecting supporter almost at the same time, and then the first of the flaming torches thrown into their midst, that people realized what was happening. A short moment of shocked silence; the screams of several of the injured, and the crowd turned almost as one on its attackers, bursting against banners flying Nazi swastikas, against emblazoned posters for the KKK, against shouts of "Burn more Jews," and against placards crying "Keep America white."

Fists flew, booted legs flailed kicks, umbrellas were wielded like swords or viciously stabbed, knives appeared, there were shots fired. Panicked police stood helplessly by until an "officer down" call brought support, first from local cops, then from the state police.

Clara, caught in the savagery and emotion of the moment and heedless, leapt down from the podium and threw herself into the melee, first wildly wielding her umbrella and tearing swastikas and placards from Nazi hands, then was swept into a packed and screaming group of protesters trying to overturn a police car.

Torches hurled by neo-Nazis showered them. One landed on the car's roof. Hands grabbed for it—Clara's too? She could never remember—the torch was thrown into the car's back seat. Flames mushroomed as it lit next to an open half-empty can of gas. In seconds the car was a cauldron of fire.

Clara, struggling to get away with others, found herself first blocked by a wall of rioters, then drawn into their midst and caught between several large attackers. Brutally struck again and again, she was finally forced to the ground with someone falling on top of her. She felt rough hands grab her arms and twist them behind her back and the sharp hurt of police plastic handcuffs tying her wrists.

There were moments after that, long forgotten but which now came back to Clara as she sat in her car, still rooted in the abandoned lot by the old mill where her follower in the dark sedan had parked, and with her looking blankly at the empty road down which it had disappeared.

There was memory of pain and blood and being piled with a dozen others, heedlessly on top of each other, into the police van and driven away from the continuing uproar; there was memory of the vehicle's siren, a piercing sound that became all embracing, eliminating nearly everything else, until it ceased and she found herself seated with others on a hard wooden bench in a cold barren room in the police station, handcuffs finally removed, arms aching and every part of her bruised and hurt and her wanting just to lie down and unable to.

There was memory too of waiting forever as the others were taken one by one to be interrogated until finally it was her turn, and she found herself in small office where there were desks and faceless, nameless police officers.

"Name? Address? Occupation? Next of kin?"

A score of other questions: why had she been there, was she part of the rally or the Neo-Nazi group? She could barely remember her numb answers only that something had happened and that her answers weren't defiant.

Not defiant, everything beaten out of her until that *thing* happened. That thing that she thought she could never erase: the probing hand between her buttocks from the officer who stood behind her; the hand that moved forward and grasped her pubis.

"Like that, girlie? I can give you something bigger and harder if you want, and let you go home without an arrest."

Laughter, and then another big hand coming around the side of her bruised body and groping her breast. "Hey, come on, girlie. Play right, and home you go. Okay?"

The hands and then her eyes on a heavy police club lying on the desktop right in front of her, her grabbing it up, wrenching her body around to face the cop, and swinging it hard across a leering face; swinging it as hard as she could swing. Once, twice.

The anguished scream of the cop, shouts, blows, handcuffs again, and the iron clang of a cell door.

After that, she remembered nothing.

TEN

The boardroom at Hanover, located in its glittering glass enclosure, was imposing, perhaps far more imposing than the importance the organization deserved. The walnut-paneled walls were graced with a half-dozen portraits of what Hanover liked to claim were the prestigious chief executives and presidents of past eras, a claim which to the knowledgeable seemed a little exaggerated since Hanover had only existed a dozen years, whilst some of the distinguished gentlemen in the portraits looking down at whomever was attending a board meeting had seen their finest day in the nineteenth century.

The long and massive highly polished

mahogany table, which saw to meetings of the board, rested securely on a thick, deeply woven carpet allowing no disturbing sound of footsteps, while those honored to be seated around it were provided with the comfort of soft leather-upholstered high-backed chairs.

To complete the decoration, heavy wall-to-wall lined drapery, when stretched across a wide window expanse, hid any boardroom event from the prying eyes of whomever might possibly strive to see in—a trepidation unheard-of to date as the boardroom was on the second floor.

Seeing the room for the first time, Ana was unimpressed. The simplicity of her life with Sven had opened her eyes to falsity in many areas, especially in such a blatant exhibition of materialism and wealth so carefully designed for a need to be superior. Uppermost in her mind was what lay behind such nonsense. Her working years as first a reporter, then an editor and publisher, had also opened her eyes to an equal falseness in people. She at once saw behind the smiling faces, the immaculate tailoring, and the manicured hands extended in welcome by the Hanover Group's representatives: Joshua Hedley, the CEO, and Armstrong Mannerworth, the president.

Hanover's two lawyers, Sam Bennington and Herb Crans, men in their sixties who were balding as well as graying, stood by with equally false smiles along with two lesser authorities, an accountant and the vice president in charge of distribution of Hanover owned newspapers. Both were unnecessary to any negotiation and clearly were there only as a show of force intended to intimidate psychologically. Their names, except for those of the lawyers, escaped Ana almost the moment they were off-handedly introduced.

Like Brad Jenkins, she was prepared for the room, the Hanover executives, and for whatever. What she was not wholly prepared for—and it came as a slight shock, which she was instantly able to hide—was the presence of none other than Arnold Speyer.

The billionaire "luminary" (his own, self-endowed expression) was seated in one of the plush board chairs, but not at the table. The chair had been removed a slight distance away so that he could play a relatively inconspicuous observer. That didn't fool Ana, nor, she hoped, Brad. Speyer, she realized, was going to play the game of a benevolent friend of the court, there as an observer to lend his wisdom to the meeting only if asked. His unexpected appearance alone made any of that cover-up laughable. Seemingly relaxed, one leg casually crossed over the other, his austere frame was cloaked as usual in expensive Italian tailoring, which ended in highly polished and fashionably tasseled moccasins. But to offset such a deliberately casual and unobtrusive presence and as though to emphasize his ultimate authority over the proceedings, his totally bald and smoothly shiny head and merciless eyes served to emphasize his famous condescension and autocratic expression that was permanently fixed on his ever-unsmiling face.

"All evil mind and nothing else," was Ana's thought when she was introduced to him, an introduction during which he seemed hardly to recognize her existence, not speaking nor rising from his chair and barely lifting his eyes from a printout he'd been reading since the moment the meeting had started.

When all were seated and further pleasantries put aside, the ice of formality was broken by Joshua Hedley. "Okay, to business," he said with a false smile. "We're here to negotiate terms of a contract that will be drawn up and signed within the next thirty days. Objections?"

"Agreed," Brad said.

"Then let's proceed. We've made you an offer to maintain *The Chronicle* financially. What's your response?"

"We've studied the contract's summary and we're prone to acceptance," Brad replied. "But with certain guarantees."

"Yes, I'm sure you have them," Hedley said pleasantly. "Can you be specific?"

Brad glanced at his notes. "Number one. Determination of subjects reported locally and the reporters' accuracy be left entirely to the judgement of *The Chronicle* editor."

"Fair enough," Hedley said. "I think we can live with that." He turned to the two lawyers. "Okay by you?"

Crans said, "Sure." Bennington smiled and nodded.

Hedley turned back to Brad. "Anything else, Brad?"

"Actual content of the paper to be maintained."

"What's your definition of 'content,' Brad?"

It was a routine question. Everyone there knew that content meant classification of reporting such as obits, marriages, church and social events, sports, fiscal reports, administration news, police and fire news, and any unexpected happenings that needed drawing attention to publicly.

Brad stoically listed them with relatively good humor, adding one or two examples for the unexpected: garage-owner Simon's wife, Heather, driving to see an accident, having an accident herself, and her car ending up on the back of Simon's tow truck along with the one it had come to salvage. And Arthur Demoine, the head in Union City of an important political party and outspoken in his views, putting in an enthusiastic supporting call to the voice mail of his state senator and discovering too late that he'd got phone numbers mixed and had been talking to the senator's opponent. When discovered, the political opposition had enjoyed a field day.

Again, a glance at the two lawyers by Hedley. Both nodded and Bennington said, "Yes, that sort of news is quite acceptable."

Armstrong Mannerworth, who up to now had been silent and hiding a condescending smile, spoke up for the first time. "What more?"

"Digital," Brad said. "And Hanover pays."

There was a brief silence. Mannerworth's smile disappeared. He took a deep breath, glanced at Hedley, who said nothing but in turn looked at the two lawyers. When they instantly assumed noncommittal expressions, and when Bennington almost imperceptibly nodded in the direction of Arnold Speyer, Mannerworth turned to look toward the tailored figure seated slightly away from the table, its phallic and shiny bald head still bent over the printout. It was unresponsive. He turned back to Brad. "That's going to be quite an expense, Brad,"

"Nonsense, Armstrong. *The Chronicle*'s presses are over seventy years old and in need of urgent repair if the paper is to be kept running. And not worth that cost as the path to them from Editorial is completely outmoded. Going digital instead of exhaustively laying print from the editors' patched-up layout would save, first, the need of major repairs, and second, pay for its installation in a year or two."

Again, an exchange of glances. Again, a lack of response from Speyer.

Mannerworth sighed. "Ok, Brad. Agreed. Digital at Hanover's expense. What's next?"

"Directors," Brad said.

"Sorry, Brad. Our choice."

"Armstrong," Brad said patiently, "that's where you're wrong. We can split them if you wish; we now run *The Chronicle* on five. But three have to be our choice. If you stop to think, it makes sense. The people who have local control over *The Chronicle* need to be the people who have an intimacy with the unique problems of the communities served which outsiders don't. And you know that as well as I do. If you want two out of the five, okay. I'll go along with that. But I repeat: three have to be ours."

A brief silence, Ana could have sworn that Armstrong Mannerworth again glanced at Arnold Speyer. She looked herself and saw no reaction. Speyer remained engrossed in the printout.

Mannerworth looked at Joshua Hedley. Hedley looked at Mannerworth. Herb Crans shrugged. Seconds ticked by, then Hadley sighed and turned to Brad Jenkins. "You've got it, Brad. Three directors to be locals, your choice. No objection."

Brad smiled. "Signed, sealed, and delivered," he said good-naturedly and, half-rising, reached across the table and shook Mannerworth's and Hedley's hands. Reseated, he said, "And lastly, before we all forget, Ana stays on as editor, as does all her staff."

"She hasn't rocked the boat in twenty years or more," Mannerworth said, gracing Ana with a faint smile. "I guess we can live with her for another twenty. That's if Ana can live with us."

Ana hadn't yet spoken, fearful of a final demand, not yet tabled, that might change the whole mood of the meeting, but she felt she had to respond to keep pleasantness going, even though perhaps for but a few minutes more. She said, "Only if you and Josh stay at the Hanover helm."

"Thank you, Ana. We have no plans to secede from the union," Mannerworth said.

"But only," Hedley added, "if I'm allowed time off occasionally to go fishing."

There was general good-natured false laughter at such a timeworn joke, and an undercurrent of relief. Then Joshua said, "Well, I guess that's just about it, everyone," and closed the file he had opened.

"Not quite, Josh, I'm afraid," Brad said. "There's one more thing."

Hedley grimaced. "Thought there might be. Go ahead, Brad."

And Ana thought, "This is it. Finally. And this one is mine." She placed a hand on Brad's arm to silence him and said firmly, "As Editor, I am to have full editorial control and responsibility."

An instant heavy silence that seemed to last forever was suddenly broken by a surprisingly high and reedy yet coldly authoritative voice that admitted no disagreement. It came from Arnold Speyer, who as he spoke still did not look up from the printout. He said, "No. Editorial control remains with Hanover and at the discretion of AAF."

Mannerworth and Hedley instantly looked grim. Any sign of pleasantness in the meeting vanished in a flash. Brad sighed and rose. "Gentlemen, if you will excuse me and Ana briefly. Ana?"

She deliberately waited, subduing her instant anger over Speyer's dictatorial stance, and letting her eyes slowly sweep everyone in the room. She was *The Chronicle*'s publisher and editor, and she wasn't going to be seen as a puppet. A silent moment or two, then she slung her handbag over her shoulder with as much dignity as she could muster and followed Brad, from the boardroom.

Closing the door of the small adjacent conference room firmly behind them, Brad slumped into a chair, and the first word he spoke was "Bastard." Ana waited as he pulled himself together. "Okay, Ana. Your choice, I'm afraid. But once more let's look at reality. We're walking on eggs. If you don't agree to surrender editorial control, the sonofabitch will almost certainly call off the whole deal. Yes, yes, I know, if we put up a fight, he just might possibly agree, thinking he'd be able to spew out his poison anyway if he let you maintain control.

"But Ana, we're not dealing with a normal person. We're dealing with a totally amoral financial killer, a man notorious for enhancing his own fortunes by ruining others. Given any excuse, such as someone standing up to him, he'd shut *The Chronicle* down just out of vindictive spite."

He paused, let it all sink in and then, with a heavy sign of unwilling resignation, said, "Ana, let the fucking bastard have his way. The issue here isn't Speyer, or you, or *any* editorial policy. The issue is continued existence of *The Chronicle*. Three small towns need local news; their merchants and producers do. Families with children do. The various clubs and churches do. They're lost without it. So, let's keep them with it for as long possible." He smiled wanly. "At least when fall comes around the kids will know who won the football game."

Staring at Brad, at his square honest features, Ana could only think what a thoroughly decent man he was and fleetingly wonder what her life would have been if they had met years ago and married. They had a secret together, from the world, from his wife. And it was his decency that made her able to be his friend and suffer from time to time only a brief twinge of nostalgia for what might have been if another woman hadn't already claimed him.

She said. "You're right, Brad, and it's all yours. I could well mess it up if I stayed, so I'm going back down to your car. Tell them I have an urgently scheduled conference call with the printer." She paused at the door. "But if you get a chance, and without ruining things, please, for me, give you-know-who a kick where it hurts most."

Driving back from Boston and the meeting with Brad, Ana felt in somewhat of a daze and silently stared out the window on her side at the passing scene of what to her, when off the Interstate, was the general roadside ugliness of billboards that announced everything from Pepsi-Cola and packaged french-fries to beauty body-lotion, shoes, and automobiles. Mentally, she was still in the Hanover boardroom with the horrid Speyer, smugly silent until the last moment, silently dominating the meeting while the others, for all their exterior appearance and mannerism of power, were all the time immersed in sycophancy and paying servile court.

She and Brad didn't talk much, even though

finally coming out of the numbness the meeting had left her in. Ana found she had little to say until they reached Union City and the diner where she had left her car, and then it was only a slightly puzzled "Where to?" as Brad drove right by without slowing.

"I think we could use a drink," he said, and came to an abrupt stop in front of the Union Pub, the local bar-grill where he silently steered Ana to a bar stool, and without delay, bought her a vodka and orange juice and had a straight vodka for himself.

After both had got their thoughts together, he said, "This has been quite a day. Small-town enterprise threatened with extinction by outside finance with nothing at all to do with the small town but everything to do with power plays and economic politics between competing greed-obsessed biggies.

"It's happening, regrettably, all over the country, not just here, and I don't see an end to it. Little guys everywhere are turning up helpless; shopkeepers, for example, run out of business by cheap buys on the internet. So if you'll allow me, Ana, I'd like to offer this thought to what I already advised at the meeting and as one step toward protecting yourself.

"I know it's little consolation, but I think the thing to do for the time being, at least, is not to even write a hint of politics in any way into your editorials. There must be plenty instead to have opinions on where strictly local events are involved, such as taking issue for some reason or other with the school board's decision on security, or complaining that the town administrator at Millstown hadn't yet presented plans for the new town septic system. Can you manage that?"

With a wry smile, Ana said she thought she probably could. She knew Brad was right. There was no use in antagonizing Speyer. That wasn't servility, the kind the Hanover Group seemed to thrive on; that was just not openly challenging someone when there was no essential need to do so.

"Send *The Chronicle* your bill," she said, half-jokingly, when she and Brad parted after he'd brought her back to her car.

"I don't bill in a situation like this," he said. "It would be like a lifeguard charging someone drowning for the preserver he tossed them." He drove off with a grin and left her, and she got back into her own car and headed for Three Rivers Junction and home, wondering at the gulf between someone like him and a Speyer.

Reaching home, Brad related the day to Kitty, then fixed himself another vodka and sat with it in silent thought, which began with curses at all the Speyers in the world and a review of the meeting, and then turned to its principal subject: *The Chronicle,* its future first, then to its publisher.

He felt far more badly about what he'd had to advise Ana than he could ever admit to her. His concern wasn't really about restricted editorial rights in *The Chronicle.* It was about Ana herself. In their brief liaison she'd told him about her family, their rejecting her and her "war," as she'd called it, and in a tone laced with bitterness how she had enlisted in the Army and suffered all war's cold reality in hope that it would give her recognition and acceptance, and how it never had. And then how she'd lost out again in her marriage.

All the misery of both had been a useless waste, a lesson in the often hopelessness of hope. And had changed nothing. But somehow, she had recovered, created a new life, and had turned into the extraordinary Ana he knew today, a woman with nerves of steel, a heart as big and generous as any he'd ever known, the deeply loyal and faithful companion to an extraordinary man everyone respected and admired, and with her become a giant when it came to running a newspaper, even though it was not a big-time one. Ana could run the *New York Times* or the *Washington Post* equally well, he thought. And as ably as anyone.

He felt good at knowing her. She and her newspaper had added something special to his life, and he could only hope that the Hanover deal and a possible betrayal by Speyer, notorious for betrayals, wouldn't lead her to a similar setback the way her war years and her marriage had.

Kitty came and sat on the arm of the chair and kissed his head. "Penny," she said.

"Thinking about the day. About old friends." He reached and took her hand, and she slid down and filled the chair beside him.

ELEVEN

～～

oming into Three Rivers Junction and waving at Simon as Simon waved to her when she drove past his garage, the stress of the day began to slip away, and Ana felt she almost couldn't wait to regale Sven with every moment that had passed in the meeting. Sven had little use for hypocrisy and even less with big banks and financiers playing monopoly with the lives of all the little people whose work had produced the money they played with.

Passing the village green and then the new church, she imagined his roars of ironic laughter. But his laughter in her ears turned to a hollow echo and then a dying whisper when, pulling up before the old church, she saw Sam Good sitting with Sally O'Donnell, the young EMT, on the front steps. Sally's presence told her at once that something was wrong. She hurriedly got out of the car. "What's happened? Where's Sven?"

And listened in near disbelief when told. Sven? But Sven was never sick. Sven was a rock. A giant tree. Everything in her screamed alarm. Boston and the meeting with the Hanover Group were instantly forgotten. All that mattered now was to get to Sven as fast as she could.

The drive on back country roads seemed forever, and when she got to the regional hospital there was inevitable further frustration in gaining admittance to the ICU to see Sven, who had been rushed to the operating theater the moment he'd arrived. Somehow keeping her wits about her, Ana said she was his sister, since only immediate family were allowed to see him, and gained admittance to the ICU waiting room. Then, after pressuring the nurse in charge, who seemed inexplicably stubborn about admitting her into the unit itself, she was finally allowed in.

Seeing Sven was an even greater shock than hearing of what had happened. Surrounded by machines with winking red lights, his deathly pale face half covered with an oxygen mask and with IV lines in both arms, he seemed strangely small and frail. Still half-unconscious after heavy anesthesia, he appeared unaware of her, and there was nothing she could do but sit by the bed and hold one of his hands in hers.

"I'm here, Sven. I'm here." It was hard to keep panic from her voice and to sound reassuring.

She was allowed but ten minutes with him, and it was only after half an hour of agonized waiting that she was able to talk to the surgeon who had operated on him.

"It was close," he said, and quickly explained Sven's suffering the often fatal abdominal aortic aneurysm and the lengthy surgical job of mending the near rupture of the major blood artery. "What happened to your brother would have killed most men his age. You have the quick action of your local EMT and our helicopter to thank for his being here at all."

Sven would have to remain a full week or more in the hospital, he said, and caution should be used in his recovery at home. "He's an unusually powerful man and looks the kind who pushes things. Don't let him. Make him take it easy for a couple of months."

Ana found words to thank the doctor and then dissolved into tears. It was the first time she had cried since flown from the war to end up at Walter Reed hospital in Washington, DC. It was there when she'd received her pardon from the Army, and was asked if she had no family to visit her, that she'd realized how terribly alone she was in the world. It was then too that isolation and failure had suddenly become unbearable; her feeling of guilt over being wounded and the soldier she'd been tending dying because she'd been too hurt to help him. It was one of the few times she could ever remember having cried.

Now, seated on a couch in the waiting room, she couldn't stop crying again and didn't try to, even though a nurse came and sat beside her with a comforting hand on hers. Sven had given her a life. She could only wonder what malicious arrow of fate had brought such a dreadful accident down on him that had nearly cost him his. And why. It was so unjust.

She could find no answer, and in an hour, she was allowed to see him again, and then waited at the hospital until the next day, sleeping wherever she could find an empty bench or a couch to lie down on, sometimes sleeping in a chair while sitting bolt upright.

Hospitals. How she hated them. She couldn't go near one without it all coming back: Walter Reed in Washington, but before it the one in Germany, and before that the field hospital that once seemed rocked by nearby explosions and where everything was pain and confusion and the shots of morphine until they gave her something else, and the fear when she awoke from surgery, the not knowing where she was or what had happened, the voices of those nurses attending her that seemed so very distant and indistinguishable. And always throughout all of it, the antiseptic smell so peculiar to hospitals and the kind of silence that sounded of noise muffled, of rubber-soled feet when a nurse came close.

Her mind kept going back. She tried to stop it—Ana, don't. It's no use. It was another life, and bad memories never solve anything. But she couldn't. Saudi Arabia, all those strange people in their robes and the women hiding everything in black except their eyes. Big ebony-skinned Smiley Grant, her medic partner in their ambulance who was always there for her when she was threatened with rape as so many other women soldiers were. Smiley taking a desperate chance, and her with him, at swigging down some scotch he'd bought from a fellow soldier who had got it who knows where.

And then they were off. Kuwait, and for her the first blinding realization that she was in a war, actually *in* one, with the roar of gunfire from the tanks that her infantry battalion followed in across the border in armored vehicles, a roar almost as shattering as the endless screech of fighter jets overhead and the chatter of Apache helicopters.

Next, Desert Storm and onward into Iraq

after what seemed only a minimum of time for rest, not days or even hours: sharing the drive with Smiley of the heavy ambulance loaded with all its drugs and bandages and stretchers and emergency gear, even body bags, through the long avenue of burned-out Iraqi tanks: the stench of still smoldering rubber and paint mingling with the sickening smell of burned-out flesh and death. Distracted only from moment to moment by Smiley's easy black laughter as he rambled about his childhood in rural Alabama: his five-mile walk to school, his rushing home fast through the village on the way because it was a "sundown" town where they lynched black men, even women, who got caught there after dark.

Dear, kind, laughing Smiley, gone forever before he could even scream from the mortar blast that hit her and the soldier they were attending, half his big dark head disappeared in a swamp of brains and blood.

The Army, going to war, hadn't eased the greater pain of uncertainty, her feeling of failure, of being a nonentity, that she had hoped it would. Yet she kept remembering it, couldn't stop until she heard the voice:

"You can see him now."

See who? Smiley? But he's gone. Smiley isn't any more.

"Miss?"

And then, waking, "Oh, my God, yes. Sven."

It was daylight, and a nurse stood over her.

He had come fully out of the heavy anesthesia and managed a weak smile when he saw her at his bedside, and said faintly, "Did you bring me some Swedish ale?" and Ana cried again. But now her tears were tears of relief, the agonizing thought of losing Sven and her life in ruins slowly fading.

It was nearly ten days before she could have him brought home in an ambulance and put to bed with emergency phone numbers for the hospital and doctors and for the helicopter service posted clearly on the wall of his bedroom along with a list of all his various medicine and pain killers.

His being an invalid meant serious changes in what had once been the simple routine of her rising early, eating breakfast, going off to work for the day, returning to make dinner, and then going to bed. Now she had to balance care of Sven with work, and the drive between the old church and *The Chronicle* at Union City, which, although not long, was nevertheless time-consuming.

She saw him settled early in the morning before she raced off, returned briefly at lunch, then was off again until her workday was over. Help came from Steve Pike who rolled in his wheelchair all the way from the new church to read to Sven and made sure he took his medicine;

and from Sam Good too, who often came from his forge to check and make sure Sven was okay and to help Sven wash and bathe and to change and launder the sheets on his bed. In two weeks' time, Sven was able to sit outside in the mornings and take brief walks while leaning heavily on Sam.

Sven's near brush with death made the bond between Ana and him even stronger. One evening while he was still in the hospital and when she had brought more fresh flowers and more Swedish ale along with his favorite brownies she'd baked especially, he had broken down and cried like a child, revealing to her the crisis in his life before he'd turned to art and left Sweden. Sitting on his bed, her arm around him, she'd heard it all: the harsh rejection by his rigid father, an elder at their church, when his love for Tove Larsen had come to light. "Boy, you're a disgrace with your vile sickness. A disgrace to our family, our guild, and our Church." And the scathing scorn of his equally religious mother as well. "Repent your wickedness, boy, ask for forgiveness in your insult to Jesus."

She heard too, and finally revealed, of the taunts and vicious attacks by his schoolmates, the pink ribbons tied to his bicycle and his school bag, the gang that had got him down, big as he was, and painted his private parts red and shaved his head too. And cruelest of all, his first illustrations that he had so painfully brought to life stolen from his school desk and smeared all over with excrement.

Only his sister, Ingebrit, had understood and lovingly offered comfort to his agony.

In a way, Ana thought, thinking back to her own family, there was a link between herself and Sven where each had found strength in the loneliness and isolation of other.

TWELVE

In her first day back in her office and impatient now to get the odious contract signed and over with, Ana found a beacon of light in Clara. In her temporary absence the young reporter had virtually taken over and had *The Chronicle* running smoothly and on time. As a bonus, there was the obituary Clara had written for Archer Meyer, which was clearly brilliant and an emotionally moving rare tribute. Ana now saw in its young writer real talent and understanding of what *The Chronicle* stood for, and realized that sitting only a few feet away from her, once more a mere reporter covering Millstown, was the unquestioned next editor and publisher of the newspaper, a woman slated one day to sit behind her big old desk, just as she had come to sit behind the desk once occupied by Ellen Brown.

She had hardly got through complimenting a nearly blushing Clara and settled down to her usual daily routine when she got a call from Brad who, after asking about Sven, dove right in.

"Have you spoken to the staff yet?"

"About what?"

"The awaited contract. What else? The onerous deal you've been forced to accept."

Ana was caught by surprise. "Do you think I should?"

"Absolutely. First, I think they have the right to know. I bet at least one will quit. And next, you need to cover yourself. You don't want some reporter coming out with an anti-Speyer sort of crack."

"I vet every edition before it goes to print."

"And never miss a bad trick?" Brad laughed. "Not ever?"

Ana surrendered. She was not infallible and had indeed missed the occasional rare mess-up in spite of the care she always took. Mistakes had to happen, like it or not. "You win," she said. "Again."

"You might need help. I'll be over at, say, nine o'clock tomorrow morning?"

Ana typed out a brief statement on her laptop and printed out a dozen or more copies: "Staff meeting at 9 a.m. tomorrow. Required attendance by everyone. No exceptions."

Passing it out, a copy on each desk in the newsroom, she avoided answering a barrage of curiosity, all of which added up to three words: "What's up, boss?"

"Nine o'clock sharp," she said, and went back to her desk, where she pretended to be at work. She dreaded telling them and realized that all the time in which she'd been totally occupied with Sven she had carefully avoided thinking about the deal she'd been forced to make, nor, especially, of the onerous horror who had forced it.

Now remembering Arnold Speyer vividly and hearing his presumptuous order all over again, she felt a little sick and was glad that Brad was coming over and had offered help, if necessary.

At five to nine the following morning, she was relieved to see all the staff, save one, were already at their desk and buzzing their curiosity amongst themselves like schoolchildren. The only person missing, bearded Billy Hicks, came through the door at precisely nine, accompanied, to her utter relief, by Brad Jenkins.

The lawyer's presence was revelation that something big might be on and caused a barely concealed sensation. Ana was relieved when he took charge. Immediately. "Good morning, everybody. Some of you may know me. I'm Brad Jenkins, and I am the attorney for *The Chronicle*. Most of you may also know, or have been affected by, various cuts in news areas that regrettably have been made recently. For example, reporting on the point-to-point races sponsored by the Meyer family at Sistine Farms, and a reduction of pages in both the Arts and Business sections. A fall-off in advertising as well as in subscriptions by many readers has come head-on with rising office expenses, your salaries, the increase cost of newsprint, printing ink, and distribution.

"A way out of this dilemma that will allow *The Chronicle* to continue publishing has been found in a forthcoming ownership of the paper that we have successfully negotiated with the Hanover Group, which owns a dozen other papers through the north country. Hanover is backed by the powerful AAF umbrella organization, which had one stipulation that we have reluctantly agreed to."

Brad took a breath to look at his expectant audience. And then said, "It's this: *The Chronicle*, neither in news reporting nor in op-eds, nor, especially, in editorials, will no longer express editorial opinion contrary to or critical of the political stance of Hanover and the AAF."

There was a momentary silence as the staff took it all in. Ana said, "Any questions? Onerous as it may seem, it was that or close down the paper. We don't have to agree, just not disagree."

Another brief silence was broken by Clara, her tone indignant, "The AAF—that's Arnold Speyer."

"Someone said, "Who the hell is Arnold Speyer?"

Forgetting herself, Clara's anger rose. "Dummy! If you don't know, start watching CNN or any other reliable news station. He's a far-right, white-supremacist, bigoted hate monger cloaked in the respectability of being a self-anointed successful businessman."

There was immediate murmuring among the other reporters. Ana, feeling like a schoolteacher, rapped on a desk and called for silence.

"We're all aware of that, Clara. Please understand that we don't like dealing with anything that has to do with Mr. Speyer; it's a little like selling *The Chronicle* south. But better keeping our paper alive than shutting it down. Speyer's part of the bargain is that we don't have to print his poison, so even if some of the bright edge has been taken off *The Chronicle*, at least folks in all three towns will be able to keep up with local goings-on. We're journalists, and it's our job in life to see that they get the news. Regardless."

"Do you think Speyer actually would shut you down if he saw you overstepping?" That was old

Spencer Warner, who had come out of retirement as a columnist to take over the far lesser task of church and obituary notices in Millstown when Clara had moved up from doing it. Ana had given him the job when she'd found out his wife of fifty years was ill and that they badly needed the money.

"You mean sneaking in opinions regardless? I wouldn't want to chance it, Spencer."

Sara Benedict, who did general reporting in Union City, chimed in. "But would the occasional overstep be chancing it, even if in error? I can't believe Speyer would be reading *The Chronicle* every week."

"He may not," Ana responded, "but he has a willing staff of sycophants whose jobs depend on their loyalty, and who knows, but it would be just our luck if the one time we overstepped turned out to be the one time only that one of them, or even Speyer himself, actually did read the paper."

"And people, they wouldn't just be looking at editorials," Brad said. "Let's be clear about that. They'd be looking at any hint of opinions in news items also."

Someone muttered, "Jesus …" And then there was a general morose silence. Until Clara spoke up again. "But, Ana," she said, and Ana could see the young woman was with difficulty trying to control rising anger, "how are we to know what is overstepping and what isn't?"

Ana sighed. She had a dull nagging sense of déjà vu. Hadn't she been in the same discussion with Brad only a few weeks ago? But with reversed roles? Then it was Brad urging reality. Now it was her doing it. "We can't know," she said, "so to avoid driving ourselves nuts, we first of all stick to straight news in our reporting, then regard the editorial column and any op-eds as being for purely local observation, like urging the town, for example, to revamp the school budget, or to audit the county recycling contract. Or," she managed a smile with the cliché, "applauding the valor of the football team."

Listening to her own words, she felt an ever vague and nagging guilt. Why? She was talking sense, wasn't she? What was there to be guilty about? She went on, "What we don't do is express any opinion about anything. Opinion even about the effect of climate change here or anywhere is a hundred percent out. And that goes for straight news reporting also, so watch what you do with personal man-on-the-street interviews. Printed, their words become ours."

"In other words," Clara said bitterly, "We're living *1984*, with the Speyers of the world on top and the rest of us in a kind of enforced submission, by never opposing their ideology, greed, or whatever."

Ana felt a surge of empathy. Until she'd come

north to Three Rivers Junction, hadn't her own life been forever toeing the line drawn by others—her family, the army, her husband? Wasn't power in the hands of a few simply an overblown extension of what most, on a far lesser scale, suffered in daily lives?

"I agree," she said, "but that's the unpleasant reality we're stuck with."

That night at home, Clara vented on Craig all the outrage that she'd carefully stifled with Ana when they talked. "It's happening all over the country," she said. "Corporate mergers and big corporations without any sense of responsibility doing everything to enrich themselves, playing big-boy games—'Hey, look at me, everyone. I *won*. I'm top dog'—regardless of any damage done to people in general. To people everywhere. People like us."

"Sure, and so what, Clara? We have a home, and a baby, and desperately needed jobs."

Clara's bitterness overflowed. "And survive only if dependent on submission to the Speyers of the world, and this Speyer in particular."

Craig had started to lose patience. "Clara, love, what do you expect Ana to do?"

"Stand up for what she believes in."

"Maybe what she believes in is her home and Sven Borg and the good *The Chronicle* does?"

"People have got to believe in more than that. Otherwise we are all lost."

"You're asking too much, Clara. If you really believe what you're saying and not just sounding off, why don't you slip in an editorial denouncing big corporate mergers and Speyer-like control of the media and see what happens."

"Maybe I will."

Petulance had crept into Clara's tone, and Craig couldn't resist laughing. Clara, he thought, had let ideology and a misplaced core of moral ethics run away with her, and his laughter concealed rising anger at her on his part. Ideology was one thing. Paying bills quite another. Had she forgotten his student loan and their need to get him started as an architect a soon as they could? "And maybe you won't," he said.

In her heart, Clara knew he'd won the argument. He was right. They were caught between a rock and a hard place, like millions of others. The Speyers of the world would win; in their case, Arnold Speyer and his control of the Hanover Group and thus *The Chronicle* where she worked.

She went silent and then answered Celine's cry in the other room, and got out a bottle from the refrigerator and put it in hot water to warm it. She had a sickening sense of doom. Whether she eventually ran *The Chronicle* as Ana had hinted or not, and because she loved her husband and child, her days of activism and protest were over. Buried forever. The rest of her life would be submission. She tried not to think that way. She tried to concentrate on feeding little Celine, so innocent of reality, on Craig and his future that would be a future for both of them, how good he was, on their little home, on her job. She tried not to think of Arnold Speyer and all the other Speyers of the world. But it was hard.

✼

The interview Clara had with Margaret Witherspoon of the League of Women Voters only a short hour before Clara's realizing that she was being followed, barely filled one column on page four of *The Chronicle*.

Margaret Witherspoon with little difficulty ignored the utter lack of interest that her husband, Horace, showed in the newspaper's failure to fill a whole page, even the front page, with the interview and not just a column in which she'd stressed to the reporter the important news of the league's latest fund-raising drive. This year it was for such a good cause, the need to emphasize English in schoolbooks in Third World countries. What was the matter with that woman who ran the newspaper? She had to be completely irresponsible. Ana Masaryk. Foreign. Probably that was it. Far better for *The Chronicle* if it were run by somebody American and more aware of what was needed in a newspaper; without question she could do a far better job herself, and often wondered how she could go about getting rid of the woman and taking over.

But glancing at her husband, who was absorbed in a soap opera on television, and even as she felt exasperation's heat rise through her bosom, she knew that lack of interest was exactly what she could expect from Horace: a lack of enthusiasm about anything of importance was the principal reason he'd never succeeded in his parents' political ambitions for him. His mother had seen him becoming president, his father in the slightly more modest role of senator. Regretfully, they had been obliged to settle for his rising only to the level of Second Selectman at Millstown, and it was clear he was going no higher, not at age sixty-five.

Conviction over the years that she had married a dead loss had become a settled fact in Margaret Witherspoon. It hadn't, however, diminished her personal ambitions and was the driving force behind her management of the Millstown branch of the league.

But perhaps, after all, Horace was right, she thought, with great reluctance. The daily work of running a newspaper was for those humdrum ordinary people who were the necessary nuts and bolts of life, not its leaders. For people like that little girl, Clara something, the reporter who had interviewed her and only thought what she'd been told as good for one column on page four.

She looked down at *The Chronicle*, which rested open to the offending page on the knees of her expensive designer housecoat. Perhaps the silly woman who ran *The Chronicle* was right too. Emphasizing English in schoolbooks in places like the Congo wasn't the most important thing in the world. That was Horace's level. The League of Women Voters had to raise money for bigger things. Something important enough to fill the front page. More importantly, to give her a legacy. She tried to think of something. Anything. And couldn't.

THIRTEEN

Two days later, when Ana came to work, she found Brad seated at her desk.

"Thought I'd save you the hike to the diner," he said.

Ana understood at once. "Today's the big day?" she said.

"Indeed, it is."

"About time. I'll let Sven know, and we're off." Ana turned to look back across the newsroom. Clara was at her desk readying to head for a day's work in Millstown. She turned back to Brad. "Unless you have any objections, I want Clara to come with us."

"Oh?"

Ana pointed to her hair. "Gray, dear man. Remember? Nobody lasts forever, and this can be partly a training exercise. She'll be taking over from me one day, I'm sure of it, and she needs to begin to think about the paper in a larger way than just reporting."

"Makes sense."

Ana went to the newsroom and Clara. "Anything urgent in Millstown today?"

"No. Just the usual look around."

"Then forget Millstown. You're coming to Boston with Brad and me."

"Boston?" Clara was surprised. "What's in Boston?"

"The Hanover Group. We're signing the takeover contract today."

"Golly. Okay." Clara managed to hide an instant twinge of anxiety that overcame surprise. Was there trouble for her in it somehow? Was there any chance she might be recognized, even if it was just her name? "Are you sure you want me along, Ana?"

Ana said, "Quite sure. Give you a first look at my job's inner workings." Ignoring a look of excitement that overcame vague consternation and which Clara was unable to hide, she waved at Brad, called Sven to tell him she was on her way to Boston, and then headed for the door.

In Brad's car, she explained to Clara, "The

austere senior businessmen you'll meet in the more-or-less imitation Versailles Palace they occupy are pawns, once independent but forced by financial circumstance to stop giving orders and take them instead. They're Hanover front men for the AAF."

Clara raised an anxious question about AAF itself. Would it be represented?

"Undoubtedly," Brad replied. "And probably Speyer with it."

"The *enfant terrible*," Ana added.

The vague anxiety Clara had felt, beginning with Ana's request she come along, increased and morphed into memories of the car that had followed her and her angry assault on the driver's window when she caught it observing her on the construction site.

At the same time, she kept hearing her husband's voice urging her to stop being paranoid. She couldn't, however, fight off the images in her mind of the stone-faced driver, and her anxiety persisted all the way to Boston, only for a moment fading at her first sight of the Hanover Group's glittering glass headquarters when they finally arrived, and then, when once inside, she found herself in the boardroom, where she was introduced to its executives, Armstrong Mannerworth and Joshua Hedley.

Both men were all ingratiating smiles and

amiability, which Clara almost at once detected as a front, as Ana had promised, and which, to a certain extent, she found laughable. She caught herself wondering what each one was really like, comparing their private lives as husbands and fathers to Craig. What sort of men were they at home and away from being big deals—if real men at all? Kind, thoughtful, miserable, weak, tyrannical? It was so hard these days for any woman to tell on first meeting, or if only knowing a man superficially. The male, she decided, seemed always to hide himself.

Little did she realize that at that very moment, Ana was having similar thoughts and inwardly cursing out the uncaring cover-up of bigness greed everywhere that seemed to have become the norm. She hated it, while at the same time realized as she watched Brad putting up a cheerful pretense with the two Hanover executives that he was far more thick-skinned than she. Brad, she knew, although a deeply caring person and one with no chip about anything, had, through law, become almost immune to being upset by the kind of situation he currently found himself in. He might deplore it, even hate it, but he didn't suffer from it, and that was the difference between Brad and herself. And more than likely between Clara and Brad, she thought, glancing at her reporter, who she saw staring past the end of the board table, and at once realized why.

Clara for the first time had spotted Arnold Speyer, and any thoughts she had about the two Hanover executives vanished instantly as Mannerworth, with considerable flourish, presented the fatal contract to be signed while Hedley was declaring to Brad, and a stoically silent Ana, what a momentous occasion it was, and what a glorious future lay ahead for the Hanover Group and its new "partner," *The Chronicle.*

Almost a parody of himself, the financier was again seated a slight distance away from all the others, and at his request hadn't received recognition on first introductions. Like some predatory animal, Speyer perversely loved to choose some dramatic moment for an unexpected entrance, until then to be silently poised and observing his victim as though awaiting the perfect moment for the kill.

And with a shock, Clara realized that as she was looking at the self-promoting famous man, he in turn was indeed staring at her. Mean, narrow little eyes drilled at her from below the well-known shiny bald head, while the face around them, in contrast, was set in a total lack of expression that in itself was somehow dangerously aggressive.

She inwardly shuddered and had just turned away to watch the contract signing, with pens hovering over paper attached with a blue ribbon and emblazoned with corporate seals, when Speyer suddenly spoke.

"Hold it." His oddly high-pitched voice, so at variance with his physical appearance, was shrill with anger. "Nothing is to be signed until the contract is amended."

Caught completely by surprise, Mannerworth and Hedley could only offer blank stares. Their two lawyers, Crans and Bennington, who had been talking to each other in low voices, silenced instantly, brows furrowed with sudden worry.

Hedley finally got out a word. "Sir?"

He was answered almost immediately. The financier left his chair and came to the table, one finger pointed accusingly at Clara. "What's that person's name?"

Mannerworth and Hedley stared blankly again. Both had already forgotten, seeing Clara as unimportant to the occasion.

Brad answered for them. "If you are referring, sir, to the young lady here, she's Clara Rosenberg."

"Does she work for *The Chronicle*?"

"Yes, sir." That was Ana. Instinctively she'd begun to bristle. "She's our top reporter."

"Thought as much. Checked on all your employees, and had her followed to be sure. Well, get rid of her. Or no deal. She's a convicted felon. Inciting to violence, attacking lawful protesters, destruction of a police car, resisting arrest, and worse, assaulting and fracturing the skull of a police officer as well as inflicting him with other serious injuries. Judge gave her three and a half years in prison. A lowlife criminal like her? It should have been ten."

FOURTEEN

There was an ensuing deathly silence. Clara had turned sheet white.

Brad spoke first, calmly but with a slight ironic laugh. "On that, gentlemen, if you will kindly excuse us, we will take a brief recess." And taking Clara firmly by the arm, he literally marched her out of the room. Ana, caught completely off guard by the outburst and revelation, silently followed a moment later, and in the conference anteroom found Brad waiting by Clara, who had collapsed in a chair, head bowed and hands covering her face.

Ana sat down opposite her. After a moment's dead silence, she said calmly, "Why didn't you tell me you'd been in jail, Clara? When I interviewed you for your job?" There was another silence, and she said, "Perhaps you'd like to explain why now, given the mess you've put me and *The Chronicle* in."

For a moment Ana thought Clara wouldn't answer. When she finally did, she dropped her hands from her face but didn't look up. Speaking, her stifled voice was a dead monotone. "I'll leave right away, Ana. I can find my own way back to Union City."

Ana, eyes still riveted on Clara, said. "That's not answering my question."

Clara had turned paler than ever, and for a moment it looked as though she was going to faint, but gripping the arms of the chair so hard that her knuckles were white, she managed to steady herself.

She didn't reply, so Ana said, "All right. I'll answer the question for you. You were frightened, weren't you? You'd tried other places for a job, I suspect, and when they found out you'd done time, they wouldn't hire you, so you decided when it came to me that you'd stay silent and hope for the best. And I was a good setup, wasn't I? *The Chronicle*'s only a short distance from your husband's hardware store."

She waited a minute. Some color had come back to Clara's face, and she looked up but avoided Ana's eyes.

"So here we are," Ana continued, "with the truth finally out in the open, and unless I give you the sack publicly back in the other room, my newspaper has had what is almost certainly its last chance at survival."

Clara had begun to cry silently, the tears running unchecked down her cheeks. "Oh, god, Ana, I'm so sorry. Please forgive me, if you can. I was desperate. So desperate."

The words then came in a jumbled rush. An avalanche. "Job. I needed a job. So very badly. Craig couldn't go it alone. And like you said, I'd been turned down by one place after another when they found out about me. Once a con, it's like you're dead, you're a leper. It was so unfair. I got fired up at the rally and then the Nazis came at us. I—I went kind of crazy, and I guess did something terrible. I don't know why. I really don't. But I did. And after we all got arrested, I only hit the cop when he assaulted me."

She choked back rising sobs and barely managed to speak a last time, and now, through her tears, said with a touch of her old defiance, "That's what they really put me away for. For refusing them sex. Nobody else was convicted. Not even the Nazis." She rose from the chair. "I'm so terribly sorry, Ana. I'm going now. And—and thank you for everything."

Ana rose too. She said, "So that's it, is it?" She

paused and added, "Well, it isn't. Brad, bring her back to the boardroom, would you please? Clara, no arguments. I'm still your boss."

She left, and Brad, again taking a surprised but numbly unresisting Clara firmly by the arm, followed.

✤

The boardroom was silent when Ana entered. Arnold Speyer had come to sit authoritatively at the head of the board table, turning angry eyes on her the moment he saw her. Mannerworth and Hedley, too terrified of Speyer to look at him, were seated where Ana had left them, both nervously fiddling with the fancy pens they'd brought to sign the contract and staring blankly at the contract itself, which lay like an offending presence before them. The two lawyers, Bennington and Crans, along with those staff members they had brought with them, stood also where Ana had left them, and at a discreet distance, their backs to the wall beneath the fake portraits of Hanover's "prestigious" founders.

Ana came to a silent halt at the end of the board table opposite Speyer. She deliberately rested her eyes a moment on the two seated Hanover executives before turning to stare at Speyer himself. Standing straight with both hands on the table, she suddenly felt that she had come to the end of a very long day. Twenty-five years had become meaningless, and now, the day nearly over, it was eventide, and night was falling, darkly ominous. Her whole being, everything of importance to her, life itself, was on the brink.

With equal deliberateness she kept silent for a moment longer before speaking, simply staring at the financier, and then said in a clear firm voice, "I have conferred with counsel, Mr. Speyer, about your demand in reference to the contract we came here to sign, and here is my answer.

"You are perhaps unaware that at an earlier age, when running a newspaper was far from my imagination, that I served with honor in the United States Army as a combat medic in Iraq. I broke discipline once, and was busted, and spent time in the lockup before I was freed and my rating reinstated. When I came out of imprisonment, the United States Army forgave my intransigency and treated me as though I had never been in. I'd paid my dues, and that was that. I was sent back to my unit and told to get to work.

"I'm one of those people, I'm afraid, Mr. Speyer, and you others who represent the Hanover Group, who firmly believes that if someone errs, and the punishment is to do time for it, that they be allowed to resume life. That includes the right to work and earn a living free from further blame.

"My reporter, Clara Rosenberg, answers just

such a situation, and I have no intention what-
soever of firing her in order to save the scurrilous
contract between us. Clara stays on. *The Chronicle*
may sink for my brashness, and I with it. In fact,
we both almost certainly will, but better we sink
honorably than surrender to the sort of cowardly
and bullying blackmail you have proposed, Mr.
Speyer. In short, sir …"

She hesitated. She wanted badly to tell him
what he could do with his deceitful contract, and
in the plain crude language she had learned in
the Army. But with the words on the tip of her
tongue, she restrained herself. She wasn't in the
Army now—the Army was in a different life and
forty years ago.

She said instead, "In short, sir, we want nothing further to do with you. We at *The Chronicle*,
Mr. Speyer, will write as we please."

Ana let that fall, and in the deathly silence
that followed, turned her back on Speyer and the
others and walked out, followed silently by Brad
and Clara.

FIFTEEN

Aaron Meyer, still immersed in sorrow at his father's death, watched with intense interest as Sam Good expertly fixed a final carefully sculpted iron shoe to the front near hoof of Challenger, a big bay thoroughbred that was his favorite jumper. Challenger wasn't easily shod, and Aaron was impressed, as he always was, with Sam's calming skill in settling a nervous horse when he worked. It had taken everything Sam had going to quiet Challenger, and Aaron, while he watched, wondered how long the elderly farrier would be able to carry on. By all rumors he was already almost ninety. And when he was gone, who on earth would replace him? There were younger farriers, yes, but far away. Situated in the north away from the mainstream of horse life, the location of the Sistine Farms stables had been his father's pick, and it was too late now, Aaron reflected, to change.

The renowned stables had become a local institution; some of its employees were from Millstown, Union City, and Three Rivers Junction. Shutting it down would be shutting off earnings for half a dozen people. Even the thought of doing that ran deeply against Aaron's grain. When he had taken over his father's life with horses, he had done so more than willingly, because that life had become his own for as long as he could remember, and his father's attitude toward wealth his own as well. "You don't own it," the older man had always said." You are only put in charge of it for a while, and that means you have a responsibility to benefit others by it also."

"Sam," Aaron asked, after Sam had driven in a last nail securing the shoe firmly to the hoof, filed away a little roughness, and then had put the hoof gently back on the ground and given the big horse a kiss on his nose. "What's local these days?" Sam was always Aaron's best source of community gossip, all the little bits *The Chronicle* sometimes missed. Occasionally, Aaron would break out a Jack Daniels, as his father had always done, and Sam would regale him with gossip for an hour or more.

"Nothing good," Sam responded.

"Oh?"

"You haven't heard? *The Chronicle*'s soon to shut down."

"It what?" Aaron didn't try to hide his surprise.

"Gone broke, I heard, like a lot of other small papers these days. Will run maybe another couple of times, and then nobody in town will know what the hell's going on any more."

"Gosh. That's a bit of a drag. Are you sure? None of my gang's told me about it."

Sam laughed. "Not surprising. Most of 'em probably figured you wouldn't care, being so far out of town and all what's going on there. I get the inside from my neighbor. That's Ana Masaryk. She's the publisher. You must know her. Comes out here from time to time; been doing so over the years to feed the horses carrots." He laughed. "Told me the other day she'd probably be asking you for a job soon."

"Ana? Sure," Aaron said, "I've known her since I was a kid and she first came up this way from New York. I showed her all over the Sistine. But Sam, that's a shame, *The Chronicle* shutting. Glad you told me."

"Guess you didn't hear about Ana and Arnold Speyer then either."

Aaron didn't try to hide instant incredulity. "Whoa! Wait a minute. Ana and Arnold Speyer? What's that all about?"

"Guess I was right. It's all over, Aaron. Seems Speyer is behind some group that wanted to put money into *The Chronicle* to keep it going, but Speyer, he said nothing doing unless Ana fired one of her reporters who once did time, so Ana upped and told the bastard where he could shove it."

"She didn't. Ana Masaryk told off Arnold Speyer? Just like that?" Aaron burst out laughing.

"Yeah, she did. God's truth," Sam said. "Sven Borg told me. And everyone's laughing just like you. People hate Speyer. But nobody's laughing about *The Chronicle* closing up. Folks want their paper to last. Same in Millstown and Union City as here. And what's that woman's name? The one who runs the League of Women Voters, or whatever it is, over to Millstown? Thinks she's better than anyone else. She's formed up a drive hoping to raise enough money to put *The Chronicle* back in business."

"That's probably Margaret Witherspoon, I guess. Married to selectman Horace and a spinsterish do-gooder from way back, if I remember right. Tried to dun my Dad for some nonsense once. Got him on the telephone and kept at him forever."

"Yeah, that's her," Sam agreed. "But a lot of folks are kicking in just the same. People's fed up with other people like Speyer running their lives. Heard even Herb Slatterly found a few gold bricks in his bank vaults someplace. I put in a couple of bucks myself. And the hotel in Three Rivers Junction done put in a hundred, and Simon's shut down his gas station a few afternoons and is running around collecting."

When Sam had gone and with Challenger back in his stall, Aaron left the stables and went to his office in a wing of the large colonial-type house his father had built only a few hundred yards away. "Whiffing all the smells horses generate is good for what ails you," Archer Meyer had always said to people who questioned the house's proximity to manure piles fueled by more than twenty-five of them.

Stopping by his young assistant, who occupied the other desk in the spacious room whose walls sported framed photos of some of Sistine's more famous horses, and before he went to his own desk, Aaron Meyer said, "Andy, write out and mail a check to Sam tomorrow, would you? The usual. I don't like to keep the old devil waiting."

He was silent a moment, shaking his head, still in disbelief at Speyer getting told off, then asked his assistant if he had on file the phone number of the League of Women Voters. "Or under the name of Witherspoon. Margaret Witherspoon."

Reaching his desk, and getting the number, he muttered, "I'll have her on my neck for years, but I guess I shouldn't be the only one who doesn't."

"What's that, sir?"

"Just talking to myself," Aaron said. He got out his cell and dialed.

In the Union City hardware store, Craig Cotswold tore himself from reading an *Architectural Magazine* and rang up the sale of a carpenter's level for a customer who wanted it to assure proper fixation of curtain rods she was putting up. When she exited the store and dropped the full change into the box at the counter end that his wife had painted up for him, he felt his usual glow of satisfaction. Bold letters amidst the artwork on the box said THE CHRONICLE, and last week Craig had turned over from the box close to $75 in contributions toward the establishment of a foundation whose aim was to assure continued distribution of the weekly newspaper to its readers in the area.

"A good thing," Craig had thought, and his opinion had been echoed by many who'd come into his store. One customer after another had virtually expressed the same sentiment as one who'd said after adding to the box, "Can't imagine not knowing what was going on around town."

Craig mentally crossed fingers that it would all keep going. That it wasn't just some sort of fad and that people would keep coming up with a dollar here, a dollar there. Whether they did or didn't, he thought at the same time, whatever happened he personally came out a winner because of the change in his wife. The endless dark moments of paranoia she'd suffered during all of the long four years since, beaten and barely seeing any point in living, she'd come out of prison, had simply ceased after the meeting she'd gone to in Boston with Ana Masaryk and Brad Jenkins, and where Ana said she'd done jail time herself when in the Army, she'd also said that she'd rather shut down the newspaper than fire Clara because she was an ex-con. Clara had kept him up half the night, crying and laughing, and telling him all about it, not once but half a dozen times, and was still awed and almost disbelieving at breakfast time.

Now he was seeing a Clara he hadn't seen since their wedding day, and perhaps not even then. Bearded Billy Hicks suspected she'd run *The Chronicle* one day, and had laughed through his beard and said, "Jail time to news time, wouldn't that be something?"

"More like architectural time," Craig thought

as he rang up another sale, and his customer dropped a dollar into the box.

✹

On her part, and once again out doing her rounds in Millstown as a reporter and staff writer for *The Chronicle,* Clara found herself realizing the futility of the activist rages that had once been her life and had ended with her being sent to prison. Continuously vivid in her mind since the moment it happened was Ana's defiance of Arnold Speyer, of Ana standing straight and proud at one end of the long board table as *The Chronicle*'s editor and publisher, Speyer waiting insolently at the other, Ana calm, the "Boss," her voice quiet, and what she said, said with dignity.

A woman whom Clara realized she'd hardly ever known, except as the "Boss," had stood up for her and for a belief in fairness and justice when the world seemed ready to end without either.

Two people had come into her life, Clara thought, when life had seemed useless, to give her the courage to go on, and she'd thought of ending it. Ana Masaryk was one, her husband the other. Craig was only a boyfriend when she'd been brought to trial all those years ago and her life seemed destroyed, and he had stood by her through all the endless accusation piled on her, one after another. He was there through the howls for vengeance by some of the press, the mobs of reporters, and the crowds struggling to get a glimpse of the "rich-girl criminal" who had ruined the life of a brave police officer, the loving husband and father of two little twin boys.

Craig could have abandoned her. Most mere boyfriends would have. The endless assault on her was so terrible. But Craig didn't. His loyalty and understanding, and above all his calm reassuring presence whenever they could be together for whatever brief moments, had somehow sustained her through the shame and humiliation of it all. In her terrible loneliness at the trial, with its cold and uncaring judge, prosecuting attorney, and unsmiling jury, the only person she knew who showed to support her was Craig. She'd been disowned by her father.

And it had been Craig sustaining her again, after the dreadful moment of sentencing, through her nearly four years in the barren jail cell as the seasons came and went with painful regularity, when her birthday and Christmas fleeted by with the only word from anyone, the phone call and whatever presents allowed prisoners, coming from him. And it was Craig when leaving prison and wearing the new dress he'd sent to her, whom she found waiting, his arms filled with flowers, to whisk her away to safety from the small knot of reporters.

Where in the past, as in the present, she had been saved when being saved was least expected, and now with most of the pain of the past effectively buried, Clara had the humbling realization that she had learned something. As her husband had shown her love, Ana had shown her a better way forward than with anger or hatred. She'd change, perhaps not quickly or all at once, but change she would eventually. And for the first time, perhaps in all her life, Clara felt a sense of calmness, even peace, within herself.

SIXTEEN

At the office of *The Chronicle*, it was well after quitting time. The staff had all gone home; the newsroom was quiet. But Ana was still at her desk taking care of the forever odds and ends that nearly every night needed to be cleaned up, and trying not to think for how much longer she'd be doing it. A month, a few weeks? Perhaps less.

People in all three towns were trying to raise money to keep *The Chronicle* alive, and that half broke her heart, for she was certain, no matter what their effort, nor for how long they kept doing it, that it would not be nearly enough. Few realized the expense of running even a small local newspaper, and the whole fund-raising drive would be a tragic waste confined to life's bitter trash bin of unresolved hopes.

Since the meeting in Boston, she'd numbly tried to ignore that defying Speyer would soon mean not just the end of *The Chronicle* but also that she'd placed herself and Sven in jeopardy; she'd endangered their home and whole way of life. With his right arm useless for illustrating, there would be no more Ophelias. She couldn't imagine doing them with anyone else and never would. Ophelia was her and Sven and her and Sven only.

The royalties for the series would soon run out, as they had from other books he'd illustrated previously. Once again in life she'd be jobless. Should she have considered that before standing up to Speyer on principle? It had all happened so quickly, and she had acted impulsively, just as she'd always done, especially in her life before coming north to Three Rivers Junction. She hadn't thought a moment before doing it, hadn't weighed any of the consequences. She'd listened to Clara and had just upped and left the conference room and without any plan, any thought, had launched straight into her refusal of the contract.

But was acting so impulsively really so bad. When you felt something deeply, shouldn't you act on it right then and there and not agonize over half a dozen options? Wasn't acting impulsively more often than not exercising your true self, the person you actually were, not the one you most often wore as a pretense, an armor against the vicissitudes of life?

Something deep inside her said yes, it was. Standing up to Speyer really had nothing at all to do with him. It had to do with herself, to not turning her back on who she really was. What was it that editor had said to her so very long ago? Something like, "Try a little defiance; stand up for issues you bring up."

Had that been the case, then, in Boston as with her whole life before it? Her being who she really was, leading her to impulsively swim against the tide of her family and their values, her impulsively joining the Army to gain recognition, and when that failed, marrying for the same reason, then taking the most impulsive leap of all—coming north to join in life with a man she hardly knew, one with whom she could never have any romantic connection, and rushing out to get a job, any job, so as to carry her share and make it work.

Ana suddenly wanted to laugh, and found herself doing so out loud. How alike she and Clara were, each for years acting impulsively, though in different ways, in seeking to escape lack of acceptance, even awareness, by others of who they were, to be allowed to be themselves.

She became aware of her little digital desk clock changing numbers. It was late; she had to get home. She began tidying up and putting things away, and tried not to think again of her newspaper's final edition. The death of *The Chronicle* was inevitable. She and Sven would face it somehow, although she had no idea how. For a start, they would have to count on Social Security; neither she nor Sven had pension plans, and savings had a way of disappearing fast. But Sven was a great cook. Perhaps they would find some way to open up a small restaurant; he'd cook and she'd wait on tables. Sam Good was soon to retire. Could they use his forge for it? "The Forge" would be a good name for a restaurant.

And if it wasn't that, there'd be another way. Just as there would be for her staff, every one of whom was a highly competent person; resilience ran deep in people. Meanwhile, there was the immediate present, and it was her duty to plod on and get the paper out for the last few times. Indeed, this very edition she had worked on all week could well be the last. The accountants would tell her on Monday.

There was a sound in the newsroom. Estella Sustino, an elderly Latina cleaning woman, was there, as she was every night, to take away trash, sweep the floor, and straighten desks the best she could. Over the years, she had sent two children born in America to college on what she had earned cleaning people's homes and toilets by day and doing the same in offices at night, and Ana's heart had always warmed to her. "There, but for the grace of God …" she'd often thought.

She finished the last of clearing her desk, and with a silent good-night as always to the portrait of Ellen Brown, rose wearily, collecting her handbag from hanging on the back of her chair and slinging it over her shoulder. On her way out of the office, and stopping a moment to speak to Estella, the office telephone rang. "To hell with it," she thought, just as Estella, always wanting to be helpful, and proud of her humble work at the newspaper, smilingly answered the call at a desk extension and said, *"Si, The Chronicle,"* then, "Please, one moment," and handed Ana the receiver.

Speaking to anyone was the last thing Ana felt like doing, but she was stuck. She took the receiver and said, "Ana Masaryk."

"Oh, Mrs. Masaryk," the caller said. "This is Margaret Witherspoon."

The road between Union City and Three Rivers Junction was narrow and dark. It was just like the other frighteningly dark road Ana had driven so many years before on her way to meet Sven in order to ask questions about finding someplace in the north to hide her messed-up unsuccessful self and the life she'd somehow always managed to fail in and to start anew. But tonight was different. Tonight, Ana felt totally unafraid.

Yesterday she and Sven had made no plans for the evening but to talk of their future. They would perhaps have to change their whole style of living, and they had both determined to put the best possible spin on it. But all that had suddenly and quite unexpectedly changed. Tonight, instead of anxiety and worry and unavoidable gloom, there would be smiles and laughter. Instead of a silent dinner, Sven would break out a bottle of Swedish Ale and she a bottle of wine. And what they would talk about, perhaps endlessly, was what she had heard from Margaret Witherspoon.

Through an anonymous donor, the League of Women Voters had received a gift. The excitedly tittering woman on the phone had refused to reveal from whom—she'd given her word not to—but the gift was very large indeed, she'd said, and it meant that now the League of Women Voters had raised enough money to keep *The Chronicle* running for a considerable time to come, with more small sums still being collected.

"We're back in business, Ellen," Ana said aloud to the beams her car's headlights threw onto the road. And then she thought, how many people had traveled this same dark road when as uncertain of their future as she had once been? What were their thoughts when they did—their thoughts and their lives, their gladness or sadness, their worries or their hopes? How many were like herself? Surely everyone, she thought. Everyone born had the always uncertainties of life to face and overcome on their way through it, just as she had.

And she thought, people when pushed down, push back up. Her defiant anti-Speyer editorial for next week would say just that when she thanked for their support all those in the three towns the paper covered: Union City, Millstown, and Three Rivers Junction. And thank, especially, the anonymous donor whose gift had put the foundation drive over the top.

The Chronicle, like so many other small local newspapers all across the nation, would continue every week to tell its loyal citizenry about themselves and to do its part in giving them a sense of pride and unity.

At the road's end, her headlights first picked out Simon's gas station, the lights of Main Street, then the Three Rivers Junction village green, its town hall and the new church, the stately overload of it all. And as finally Ana saw the two little carriage lamps lighting the front door of the old church, that was her home and where, prepared by Sven, dinner awaited, her spirits soared.

Ahead, an evening with Sven, and tomorrow, another busy day at the office, when she had a newspaper to assemble for delivery of its regular weekly edition the day after.

End

EPILOGUE

*T*he following editorial appeared in the next issue of *The Chronicle*.

We live in troubled times. Climate change threatens all future generations, a fragile economy teeters under the weight of polarization, civil communication between us falters before onrushing vulgarity, anger, and hate. And we are daily faced with insidious unity among forces we seem helpless to resist: giant corporations merge, heedless of the effect on their workers; government under the influence of money often legislates on behalf of a limited few while ignoring the best interests of all; and autocratic individuals, striving ceaselessly for power through demagoguery while ignoring every law, erode universal liberty. These are forces that minimize us daily, and too often even crush us.

We in Three Rivers Junction, in Millstown, and in Union City, like so many across our great nation, find it ever harder to maintain the standards and relative freedoms that our parents often took for granted. Yet we have a voice to push back against those forces that would lessen our heritage, a voice to fight for economic independence, a voice to fight for what is in our best interest and best for us. That voice, besides at the ballot box, is amplified by the force of our media, both national and local.

Recently Mr. Arnold Speyer's All-American Freedom, or AAF, chose to take away our voice in our three towns by shutting down *The Chronicle* and employing a fabricated excuse to do so that belied all concept of fairness or justice. But you, the citizenry of all three towns, weren't having your mutual voice stilled. You resisted, and your resistance in defying Mr. Speyer showed the kind of courage and determination that often lies unnoticed in the breast of the common man. You were pushed down, but from piggy banks to pocket money and to the most generous checking account of an anonymous donor amongst you, you stood up and fought back.

You will be rewarded. But your reward won't come from the halls of Congress or the White House; your reward will come from the sense of unity you will have amongst yourselves and from being reliably informed of events critical to your daily lives: events that mark the births and deaths of your fellows, reports of local disasters or successes, information as to what your chosen leaders are doing to benefit your lives, or what they are not doing.

In the satisfaction David felt when he fought and conquered Goliath, you will be rewarded. You are heroes, all of you. And may God bless you as you have blessed your weekly local newspaper, *The Chronicle.*

Ana Masaryk,
Editor and Publisher

ABOUT THE AUTHOR

Born to wealth and privilege in New York, David Osborn chose to spurn both as false icons after World War II combat as a Marine Corps dive bomber pilot. On his own and following brief careers in television and public relations, he expatriated to France when falsely accused of un-Americanism in the infamous Senator McCarthy era, paying his way with a co-authored first motion picture script, *Chase a Crooked Shadow*. When its star-studded success took him from laboring in a rock quarry in France into Britain's film industry, he was launched on a long world-class writing career that saw him dangerously engaged during several Cold War years with Czech anticommunist resistance behind the Iron Curtain. Living in France and England as well as isolated for twelve years in a tiny Alpine village in Switzerland, Osborn authored numerous stellar TV plays and a score of major motion pictures, including *The Trap*, which earned an Academy Award nomination. Turning novelist with the critical success of *The Glass Tower* followed by the world best-selling classics *Open Season, The French Decision, Love and Treason,* and a half dozen more outstanding thrillers, he has had many imitators, but none reaching the startling originality of his stories, the stunning impact of his flawless page-turning plots, and his literate prose in each that packs a powerful punch with nearly every line.

ALSO BY DAVID OSBORN

Novels and Screenwriting

Novels

The Glass Tower – Hodder & Stoughton
Open Season – The Dial Press
The French Decision – Doubleday
Love and Treason – New American Library
Heads – Bantam
Murder on Martha's Vineyard – Lynx
Murder on the Chesapeake – Simon & Schuster
Murder in the Napa Valley – Simon & Schuster
The Last Pope – Source Books
The Cape Cod Blue – Dagmar Miura
Alicia's Secret (young adult) – Dagmar Miura
A Cold Wind from the Andes – Dagmar Miura
The Head Hunters – Dagmar Miura
Looking Back: The Long Life of a Writer (a memoir)
Delta Red – Dagmar Miura
Eventide – Dagmar Miura
The Somersville Bodies – Dagmar Miura

Cold Case 369 – Dagmar Miura
The Lighthouse (a novella)– Dagmar Miura
The Saugatuck Conspiracy – Dagmar Miura

For Children

Jessica and the Crocodile Knight (a novel)
– HarperCollins

Jessica and Her Adventures in Fairyland (collection
of five novellas) – Dagmar Miura

Ophelia and Her Forest Friends (series of ten stories)
– Dagmar Miura

Jessica and the Witch's Broom – Dagmar Miura

Jessica and the Flying Unicorns – Dagmar Miura

Jessica and the Golden Swan Feather – Dagmar
Miura

Feature Films

The Trap (original story and screenplay; Academy
Award nominee for Best Foreign Film)
– Columbia

Open Season (screenplay, adapted from Osborn's
own best-selling novel *Open Season*)
– Columbia

Chase a Crooked Shadow (original story and
screenplay co-written with Charles Sinclair;
listed by the British Academy of Motion
Picture Science as "One of the ten best
suspense scripts ever written") – Warner Bros.

Moment of Danger, a.k.a. *Malaga* (screenplay
adapted from the novel) – Warner Bros.

Malaga (screenplay) – Warner Bros.

Maroc 7 (original story and screenplay) – J. Arthur Rank

Deadlier Than the Male (original story and screenplay) – J. Arthur Rank

Some Girls Do (original story and screenplay) – J. Arthur Rank

The Road to Dusty Death (screenplay) – J. Arthur Rank

The Games (screenplay) – Associated British

Follow the Boys (original story and screenplay) – MGM

Beat Girl (original story and screenplay) – Renown Films/British Lion

Stop-over Forever (original story and screenplay) – British Lion

Winter Holiday (original story and screenplay) – MGM

Penny Gold (original story and screenplay) – J. Arthur Rank/Columbia

Whoever Slew Auntie Roo? (original story and screenplay) – Paramount & American International

Murder, She Said (screenplay, Agatha Christie adaptation) – MGM

Murder at the Gallop (screenplay, Agatha Christie adaptation) – MGM

Feature-Length Documentaries

Fangio, The History of Formula One Racing (original screenplay; executive producer) – Volpi Productions

Why Ireland – Irish Tourist Bureau

Films Canceled While in Production

HMS Ulysses – Volpi Productions (screenplay adaptation of the Alistair MacLean novel about protecting North Sea convoys to Russia during World War II; production halted when a key warship was unavailable)

The Mad Motorists – Volpi Productions (screenplay adaptation from the Allen Andrews novel about the 1907 Peking to Paris race)

Eagle at Sundown – Dragon Films (original screen story about Napoleon's escape from Elba; starring Douglas Fairbanks; in production when canceled)

Les Petits Rats – Disney (original story and screenplay about the Paris Ballet school; production begun, then canceled)

Hunters' Horn – McCahon Productions (screenplay adaptation from the Harriette Simpson Arnow novel; production canceled; financing failure)

Blood on the Rose – British Lion (screenplay adaptation from the Phyllis Hastings novel)

Television

Bouquet for Miss Olive (three-act play; British Television Producers Association nominee for Best Play of the Year) – Granada/ITV

Three on a Gas Ring (three-act play; British Television Producers Association nominee for Best Play of the Year) – Granada/ITV

Why George Brown Hanged (three-act play) – Granada/ITV

Arthur of the Britons (pilot and three scripts on the life of King Arthur; Writers Guild of Great Britain award winner for Best British Children's Series)

The Antiquers (original story, pilot, and six episodes in the sitcom series) – Irish National Television

9 781951 130138